8/15

S0-ARM-220

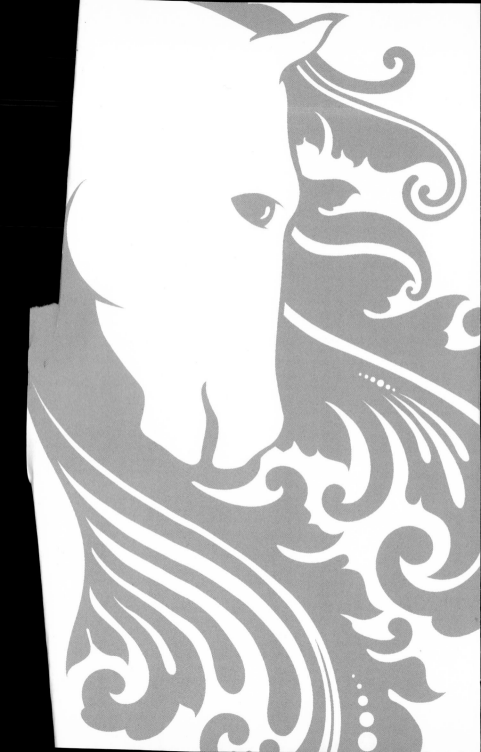

Sable Hamilton

STARDUST STABLES

Wildfire

East Bridgewater Public Library
32 Union Street
East Bridgewater, MA 02333

STONE ARCH BOOKS
a capstone imprint

Stardust Stables is published by Stone Arch Books
A Capstone Imprint
1710 Roe Crest Drive
North Mankato, Minnesota 56003
www.capstonepub.com

First published by
Stripes Publishing Ltd
1 The Coda Centre, 189 Munster Road
London SW6 6AW
Text © Jenny Oldfield, 2013
Cover © Stripes Publishing Ltd, 2013
Stock photography © Shutterstock, 2013

All Rights Reserved.

No part of this publication may be reproduced in whole or in part,
or stored in a retrieval system, or transmitted in any form or by any
means, electronic, mechanical, photocopying, recording, or otherwise,
without written permission of the publisher.

Library of Congress Cataloging-in-Publication Data is available
on the Library of Congress website.

ISBN: 978-1-4342-9791-4 (library binding)
ISBN: 978-1-4342-9795-2 (paperback)
ISBN: 978-1-4965-0207-0 (eBook PDF)

Summary: While Alisa and Diabolo work as stunt doubles on the set
of an adventure movie, things at Stardust are getting tense.

Designer: Alison Thiele

Artistic Elements: Shutterstock

Printed in China.
092014   008472RRDS15

For Shelley, my fearless friend

Chapter 1

"Alisa, where are you?"

"In here, with Diabolo!"

"Where? I can't see you!" Kami Cooper stepped out of the bright sunshine into the cool shadows of the old red barn at Stardust Stables.

"Here!" Alisa appeared from behind the grain store carrying a scoop of pellets for her horse. "Diabolo worked extra hard for me today."

Back in the row of wooden stalls that lined one side of the barn, the sorrel mare poked her head over a sturdy partition and nickered hungrily.

"I've been sent to tell you that supper's ready," Kami told Alisa. "But I should've known you'd feed your horse before yourself!"

"Of course," Alisa replied. She took the feed and poured it into Diabolo's manger. A shaft of sunlight put rich auburn highlights into her long, dark hair and brought out the soft glow of her lightly tanned face.

"Isn't she gorgeous?" Alisa murmured as Diabolo crunched the pellets.

"She sure is. Anyhow, it's time for our supper. We're having a cookout by the creek," Kami reminded her. Even though she and Alisa were roommates, Kami still felt a little shy around her. She'd only been part of the Stardust stunt-riding team for a few weeks, but Alisa had spent three summers at the stable. She had the reputation of being the best junior rider in the business.

"The white patch down her face — isn't it just perfect?" said Alisa with a contented sigh, showing she was still focused more on Diabolo than the cookout.

Kami tried again. "Alisa, Lizzie sent me to tell you — you need to put your steak on the grill."

"What? Oh, yeah." Alisa sighed then walked into the stall, ready to lead Diabolo out into the meadow. "I'll be right there."

"Do you want me to cook it for you?" Kami offered. She knew just how in love Alisa was with Diabolo — she felt exactly the same about her horse, Magic. "How do you like it — medium rare?"

"Sure," Alisa agreed absent-mindedly.

"It'll be ready in ten," Kami said as she turned and headed back to the cookout. "Don't be late or one of the boys will eat it for you!"

Alisa ran her hand down Diabolo's smooth neck and through her silky mane before buckling on a halter and attaching a lead rope. "Come on, it's time to get you out to pasture."

The mare clip-clopped out into the corral, then stopped dead. "Okay, I know you don't need this rope," Alisa agreed as Diabolo dug in her heels and tossed her head. She unbuckled the halter. "You're a big girl — you can walk there all by yourself. But you do need me to get the gates."

Freed from the lead rope, Diabolo waited patiently for Alisa to pull the tall metal lever and for the first gate to swing open. Then she walked through, her chestnut brown coat gleaming, long tail swishing. Gate number two would give her access to cool water from Elk Creek and to the meadow beyond. She waited while Alisa released the second catch and then walked to the water's edge. She paused again, raising her head to smell the smoke from the barbecue further upstream.

"Go!" Alisa urged.

Diabolo glanced back at her and blew out through her lips.

"Go eat some grass!"

At last, with a toss of her head, Diabolo stepped into the creek and waded across. Alisa watched her as she reached the far bank, launched into an easy trot, and joined the other horses grazing in the meadow. Then Diabolo turned and whinnied as if to say, *"Your turn now — go eat!"*

Alisa laughed. "Okay, I hear you. I'm out of here."

But she stood there just a little longer, reflecting on the great day she had had working with Diabolo in the round pen on vaults and saddle falls. Her wonderful, talented horse hadn't made one mistake. Lizzie had praised her, and Jack, co-owner of Stardust Stables with Lizzie, had told her there would soon be feedback from the *Wildfire* audition they'd done a week earlier.

"You'll get the job, no problem," Kami had assured her earnestly.

Jack had agreed. "They'd be crazy not to want you and Diabolo for that movie."

"Let's hope," she said out loud as she came back into the present. She started walking across the yard to join the others at the cookout. She smelled barbecued steak and heard people laughing and having fun. "But first, let's eat."

∽ ◦ ⌒

Slabs of meat sizzled on the grill under Tom's careful watch. Zak came around with a bowl of fruit punch. "More?" he said to Hayley. Hayley quickly gulped down the remaining contents of her cup. Then she nodded and held it out.

"Sooo thirsty after all those saddle falls!" she croaked. "I got dust in my throat, up my nose, and you don't even want to know where else!"

"Yuck!" Alisa said, putting her hands over her ears.

"So, how come you don't eat dirt like the rest of us?" Hayley asked Alisa. She put her cup down and untied her long braids, shaking out her hair.

"I do," Alisa protested.

"You don't look like you do," Hayley said. Although only thirteen, she'd been a junior stunt rider at Stardust for the last couple of years.

"She's right," Kellie agreed as she sat down beside them. Kellie, Hayley, and Alisa were the some of the most successful riders on the team. Now Kami was more than happy to join them. "Alisa, you could fall from your saddle, roll on the ground, and still jump up looking like you just stepped out of the Wrangler store, all crisp and shiny."

"Look at me!" Hayley wailed as she scrubbed at dark patches of mud on her pale blue shirt. She beat dust from her jeans and swatted her Stetson against a tree trunk. "I take one fall from Cool Kid's saddle and look what happens."

"That's because Diabolo's so smart she knows not to dump me in the mud." Alisa laughed. "She's real gentle with me."

"Anyone want more rib eye?" Kellie's brother, Tom, yelled from his station behind the barbecue.

Alisa noticed that Kami was first in line and smiled at her roommate's eagerness.

Kellie saw it too. "I know," she muttered, raising her eyebrows. "Ever since they got back from the *Moonlight Dream* job in California, my brother and Kami have been joined at the hip."

"It's cute," Hayley insisted. "But she's so tiny and skinny, I have no clue how she can eat so much food!"

The three girls sat cross-legged in the long grass, enjoying the cool evening. They watched the last of the sun as it sank behind Clearwater Peak.

"So, do you know yet — did you get the *Wildfire* job?" Kami asked Alisa as she joined the gang. She sat on a fallen tree and stretched out her legs.

"We still haven't heard. I've got my fingers crossed, though."

"You'll get it," Kami and Hayley chorused.

"Keep the faith," Kellie added.

All the stunt riders at Stardust knew that Jack and Lizzie Jones were really hoping to get a yes from Diamond Studios. Contracts were like gold these days. Although the owners never discussed it openly, everyone knew that the business was struggling ever since Lizzie's ex-husband, Pete Mason, had set up High Noon Stables, a rival stunt-riding school, just up the highway.

"Look at what you've done already," Kellie reminded Alisa. "Last year you did all the stunt riding for Jaime Matthews in the *Desert Horse* series. The year before that you doubled for Jessica Lawson in that rodeo movie."

"Bronc Rider," Zak reminded them. "Everyone knows you're at the top of your game."

Alisa took the compliments with a modest smile. "Thanks, guys. Diabolo was fantastic at the *Wildfire* audition, the same as always. But there are no cast-iron guarantees."

She sat in the lengthening shadows, remembering the day a week earlier when the *Wildfire* director, Mike Peterson, and his head wrangler, Rex Boyle, had driven down to Stardust Stables from the set in northern Colorado especially to see her ride Diabolo through fire.

Every second of the audition was still etched in her brain.

∽ ⊙ ⌒

"This is Alisa Hamilton." Lizzie made the introductions. A nervous Alisa shook hands with a tall, lean, weathered-looking guy who turned out to be Rex Boyle, the guy in charge of equine stunts for *Wildfire*. Then she met an equally tall but chunkier guy with more of an indoors look. He was Mr. Peterson, the director.

Peterson scrutinized Alisa from head to toe but said nothing.

Rex was the one who checked out Diabolo and asked all the questions. "How does the horse act around sheer cliffs and ledges?"

"Good — she's totally used to it," Alisa assured him. Her mouth was dry, her legs shaking a little from nerves. She was glad when Kami paused her work with Magic to come and wish her luck.

"You can do this," Kami murmured.

Alisa smiled and nodded.

"How about forest trails?" Rex asked.

"Good again."

"And the big question — how does she deal with flames and smoke?"

"Diabolo is great around fire." Lizzie stepped in to convince the men that she and Jack had chosen Alisa and Diabolo to audition for exactly this reason. "Most horses hate it. Their instinct is to run — you know, fight or flight. But not Diabolo."

"Horses generally fall into the flight category," Rex had explained to the director.

"Canines, bears, big cats — they fight when they encounter danger. Horses are hard-wired to run away from it. And nothing comes higher on their list of dangers than fire."

"So finding a horse who's willing to stick around when we set a controlled fire on the mountain — that's a rare thing?" asked the director.

"Yes, sir," Rex confirmed.

Alisa stood between Diabolo and Kami. She listened carefully, growing more nervous by the second. They could talk all they liked — the only way to prove that Diabolo was the horse they needed was for her to demonstrate it.

Seeming to read her mind, Lizzie suggested a trial run. "We've trained Diabolo to ride through blazing arches," she told the visitors. "My husband, Jack, has set everything up. Would you like to see?"

A nod from both Rex and Mike Peterson set things in motion. Alisa took a deep breath then jumped nimbly into the saddle, while Jack, Kami, and Tom got to work inside the round pen, checking the six-foot-high square arches. They were built from two wire columns and a crossbar, all wrapped with fabric soaked in paraffin. Six arches with that same set up were arranged around the rim of the pen. With a word from Jack, Tom and Kami stepped aside. Jack set the arches on fire.

Alisa heard the whoosh of flames igniting.

"Okay, let's do it," Alisa murmured into her horse's ear, seeing orange flames reflected in Diabolo's dark eyes. She eased her forward. "You know how this works. We launch straight into a flat-out gallop, then we run under those arches, no questions asked!"

Alisa pressed her heels into Diabolo's sides and sank deep into the saddle. She saw the flames, heard them pop and crackle, smelled the acrid black smoke. Still confident that Diabolo would override her instinct to turn and flee, Alisa asked her to go ahead.

The sorrel mare sat deep on her haunches and launched herself at the first arch, mane and tail flying. As she galloped through the flames,

Alisa's nerves suddenly settled. She crouched forward like a race jockey, urging Diabolo on. They took the second and the third arches without hesitating. There were one, two, three blasts of heat — smoke stung their eyes and the whole world seemed to be burning around them. But on they went, through arches four and five, still not pausing for breath until they'd made it under the sixth arch and slid to a halt right by the gate where they'd started.

"Good job." Rex didn't seem like a guy who was free with compliments, but even he was impressed. "It was totally worth the drive down from Estes Park."

Kami heard the comment and gave Alisa a high five. Tom, too, congratulated her with a wide smile and thumbs up.

"Do you want to see anything else?" Lizzie asked. "Alisa can show you any number of stunts: saddle falls, vaults, hanging from the saddle, front wings, vertical wings —"

"No, we're done," Mike Peterson said abruptly. His face was deliberately set in an expression that gave nothing away. "We have to move on to the next stable; what's it called?"

"High Noon Stables, just south of Colorado Springs," Rex reminded him.

Alisa's heart sank when she heard the name, and she could tell that Lizzie and Jack felt the same. Kami and Tom also looked worried by the news.

"We have more riders to audition there," the director explained.

"So, when will you be able to let us know?" Jack's question was a split second too soon and too eager. He confessed later he'd almost bitten his tongue off for showing how much the job meant to everyone at Stardust.

"In a week," Rex promised as he followed Mike Peterson back to their car.

Relieved that the stunt had gone well, Alisa slipped down from the saddle and led Diabolo away from the round pen where the burned arches still smoked.

Halfway across the yard, Diabolo nudged her arm as if to say, *So how did we do?*

Alisa looped her arm around her horse's neck and buried her face into her long nut-brown mane. "We did the very best we could," she told her. "Now we just have to wait and see."

∽ ◦ ⌒

"How good is this steak," Kami mumbled,

breaking into Alisa's action replay of the audition and bringing her back to the present.

"Good," Alisa agreed.

"How lucky are we!" As a pale crescent moon rose in the dusky sky and the creek water burbled at their feet, Kellie voiced what everyone was feeling. "Just to be here — all of us together, working with some of the greatest horses, being taught by such totally cool trainers, getting to meet the biggest movie stars . . ."

Hayley, Kami, and Alisa all smiled. It was true. They were living the dream out here in the Rocky Mountains, under the vast, blue Colorado sky.

"And with hunks like Tom around, it's just the icing on the cake!" Hayley quipped, nudging Kami in the ribs.

Kami felt a hot blush cover her face. She had a strong bond with all her fellow stunt riders, but especially with Tom. His smile made her feel special and made her heart beat faster whenever they were together. She prayed that he was too far away to overhear their conversation.

"It's true looove!" Hayley crooned.

"Hush, don't talk so loud!" Kami pleaded.

"Yeah, Hayley! Give Kami a break," Alisa said, while Kellie clamped her hand over jokester Hayley's mouth.

"Urgh, this is my brother we're talking about, remember!" Kellie protested as the two girls rolled backward down the slope.

As they clambered back up, they saw Lizzie Jones appear at the door of the main ranch house and stride across the grass toward them. Her black Stetson was tilted far down over her forehead, her black shirt was neatly tucked into her Wrangler jeans, and her fancy silver belt buckle gleamed in the evening light.

"Looks like she has some news to share," Kami observed.

Was Lizzie smiling or serious? The girls couldn't tell because of the shadow cast by the brim of her hat.

"I bet it's about your audition," Kellie predicted, holding up both hands and crossing her fingers.

Alisa held her breath. Was it good news or bad?

"I just got a phone call from Rex Boyle," Lizzie said. She paused.

Zak and Tom joined the group. "And?" Zak prompted.

Lizzie tilted her black hat back to reveal a broad smile.

"Alisa and Diabolo got the *Wildfire* job! It's

all happening fast. Alisa — you start work tomorrow."

"Yes!" Kami, Kellie, and Hayley high-fived while Zak rushed over to Alisa and lifted her off her feet.

"This is fantastic news," Lizzie told them. "Alisa, I'm so proud of you!"

"This is a big, big movie!" Kami gasped, her admiration for Alisa soaring higher than ever. "I knew you would get the role. I just knew it!"

"Me too!" Kellie echoed, while Zak stood back, blushing at having just lifted cool and elegant Alisa clean off her feet.

Still smiling, Lizzie took Alisa's hand. "You'll be such a good ambassador for Stardust," she assured her. "Up there in Estes Park, working with Rex and Mr. Peterson — you and Diabolo will be total stars!"

Chapter 2

That evening Alisa left the cookout early and headed for the tiny bedroom she shared with Kami in the girls' dorm next to the main lodge.

"Are you leaving already?" Tom called after her from his station behind the barbecue, where he was busy cooking second helpings of steak. He brandished the sauce bottle, aiming at Alisa and threatening to shoot.

Glancing over her shoulder, she grinned. "Don't even think about it. Anyway, unlike you guys, I have to get up before five tomorrow to get to Estes Park."

"Jeez, she's so grown up," Hayley groaned. "Me — I'd want to stay up all night and party!"

"Alisa was born responsible." Everyone turned to see latecomer Becca grab a paper plate and take a steak from the grill. She was just back from filming a commercial for a vitamin company called Equivit with Pepper, her gray Quarter Horse. Unlike Kellie, Kami, and Hayley, Becca wasn't a fan of Alisa's.

"Responsible meaning boring?" Kami asked with a frown. She didn't like anyone aiming unfair criticism at Alisa.

"Yeah, look at her — being a party pooper instead of celebrating."

"Becca, you're so mean," Kellie protested. She had worked alongside Alisa for two summers and, like Kami, she looked up to her.

"No, I'm not." Becca set her mouth in a stubborn line. "I'm being honest. When did you ever see Alisa let her hair down?"

"Plenty of times," Hayley cut in. Alisa might have been way more sophisticated than the rest of them, but that didn't stop her from having fun.

"Like when?"

"Like when she lopes Diabolo in the creek," Kellie suggested. "She's always out there in front, whooping and yee-hahing."

"Or in the round pen," Hayley added. "Who's the biggest daredevil in our barrel-racing competitions?"

"Alisa," Zak confirmed.

And as they all watched their rising star vanish into the dorm, Kami surprised herself by being the one who stepped in before Becca could come up with any more sly digs. "Plus, she's the most exciting stunt rider you're ever going to see," she said. "So anyone who tells me she's boring is saying more about themselves than about Alisa."

"What do you mean?" Becca asked.

"I mean that person is just plain jealous of Alisa's riding ability," Kami insisted.

Everyone stared at her. She blushed.

"The mouse roars like a lion!" Zak laughed. "Right on, Kami — you go, girl!"

∽ ◦ ⌒

But what you saw was not what you got with Alisa.

Sure, she knew the others viewed her as cool and confident, calm and collected. After all, they playfully teased her about it all the time, as well as about her immaculately ironed shirts and glossy dark hair.

What they didn't know was how she truly felt inside. *I'm fourteen — still just a kid!* she wanted to tell them. *I freak out with nerves and I never think I'm good enough, just like all of you.*

Sighing, she closed the door on the outside world and stared at herself in the mirror propped up on her bedside table. "Get a grip," she said firmly. "The *Wildfire* job is yours — you earned it with blood, sweat, and tears."

She thought back to all the hours, weeks, months, and years she'd put into perfecting her horsemanship; how, even as a young kid, she would constantly beat herself up for anything less than perfect results.

"That's your problem, you're too much of a perfectionist," her worried mom would tell her, back home in North Carolina. The family didn't have much — no big house with a swimming pool and flashy car, just a piece of land in the foothills of the Blue Ridge Mountains. Her dad bred and raised livestock: mainly cattle and horses.

"Pursuing perfection is not a problem," her ambitious dad would argue back. "Alisa needs to work hard to carve out a life of her own."

She had taken him at his word and honed her riding skills until there was nothing she couldn't jump on horseback, no race she couldn't win. By the age of ten she was competing in barrel-racing and reining contests. By twelve she was at intercounty level. Last year she'd even entered Bonnie, her beloved dark bay Quarter Horse back home, into a reining competition held in the neighboring state of Virginia, where they'd come second to Lucy Reeves, a fifteen-year-old national champion and Olympic hopeful.

"Second prize," she had told her dad over the phone.

"Good job," he'd told her. "Second is something, anyway." But she'd been able to tell straight away by the flat tone of his voice that he was disappointed.

She'd gone home and worked with Bonnie even harder than before.

Now, with a last look at herself in the mirror, Alisa reminded herself that she and Diabolo had an important job to do in the morning. She took a clean pair of jeans and a shirt out of a drawer and laid them over the back of a chair. Then she polished her boots. After this she ran through the list of tack that she would need to pick up from the tack room: Diabolo's bit and bridle, clean saddle blanket, girth and saddle, plus halter and lead rope. Lastly she undressed and took a shower before getting changed for bed. She was ready to switch off her light when Kami came into the room.

"What time did you set your alarm?" Kami asked, sitting on her bed, ready to chat.

"Four-thirty."

"You want me to set mine, too?"

"No, thanks. I'm sure I'll wake up. I always do when I've got a job. Tomorrow's going to be a busy day. Jack and I have a two-hour drive up to Estes Park and then a whole day of meeting people on the set, reading through the script, and walking through the action. We might even shoot a scene before we make the drive back home."

Kami blushed as she spoke. "Alisa, I was thinking — I hope you don't mind . . ."

"Come on, spit it out — you know I won't bite."

"Do you think I could come with you tomorrow, just for the ride?" Kami said in a rush. "Then I could see the movie set and get a whole lot more information on how this business operates, plus I could help Jack and you with any chores."

"I don't see why not," Alisa said, almost before Kami had finished her sentence. "You just need to check with Jack to see if it's okay."

"You're serious?" Kami's grin broadened. "I mean, that would be so cool. You're sure you don't mind?"

Alisa smiled back. "Not at all. I totally want you to come."

Kami let out a long sigh. "Thanks, Alisa.

Not just for this, but for everything. You, Kellie, and Hayley — you've all been so nice to me, so welcoming ever since I started here."

"No problem. We happen to think that you and Magic make a great team."

"No, seriously — the first couple of days I was really homesick. But you, Kellie, and Hayley got me through that with chats around the soda fountain and rides along Elk Creek. You made me feel like I belong."

"You do," Alisa assured her. "That's why it'll be great to have you along tomorrow. You'll have to be up early, though."

"I'll be there!" Kami promised, jumping up to run and find Jack, but she remembered something and came back into the room. "Oh, I forgot — Tom and Zak told me to wish you luck."

"Okay, thanks." Alisa was pleased to hear that the boys were thinking of her.

"They said for you to stay calm, not to be too nervous."

"Easier said than done." She already had butterflies in her stomach, like always. "But I'm more excited than scared, I guess."

"So we're all good?"

"All good. Honestly, Kami — I'm really looking forward to tomorrow."

"Me too." Kami gave her a quick, bright smile. "You go ahead and get some sleep," she said as she pulled the door closed. "I'll try not to wake you when I come to bed. I promise!"

Chapter 3

"Ready?" Jack asked Alisa and Kami next morning.

The sun hadn't risen and there was a strange gray, pre-dawn light in the sky as the girls climbed into the cab of the trailer.

"Yeah, let's go," they replied.

Tom had been there to help them load Diabolo, along with all the tack they would need for their first day on the *Wildfire* set. Alisa could hear Diabolo's hooves clunking on the metal floor of the trailer as she settled in for the drive to Estes Park.

"You put a hay net in there for her?" Jack checked with Kami, who was buttoned up in a denim jacket against the cold morning air.

"Yep."

"You got the brushes and currycombs?"

"Check."

"Okay, let's go." He started the engine and eased the trailer out of the silent yard.

Alisa and Kami waved goodbye to Tom and then glanced back at the meadow, where they could make out Dylan, Magic, and Cool Kid feeding from the iron rack that Tom had already loaded with fresh alfalfa. Other horses were crowding around, too — Legend and Ziggy, together with Pepper, all jostling for position.

"This is kind of nice," Jack commented as he turned on the radio and mellow country music filled the cab. "We leave early and we get back late, but at least this movie is being shot close to home. It means we get to sleep in our own beds at night."

"Do we know any more about who I'm doubling for?" Alisa asked.

Jack braked to avoid a mule deer and her baby that had leaped out of the thorn bushes onto the side of the dirt road. He let them safely cross, then drove on. "Lizzie spoke to Rex Boyle again late last night. Hannah Hart is playing the young lead. You two look alike, so you'll be doubling for her in the big action scenes."

"Cool!" Kami had seen Hannah's face in magazines and knew all about her. She was the hot young star of the moment, always attending celebrity parties, usually on the arm of another actor or a rock star or some teen sensation. She was also a talented actress who, at the age of fifteen, had acted alongside some of the world's top movie stars.

"Hannah is actually a pretty good rider herself, so Diamond Studios is happy to let her do some of her own stunts on one of Rex Boyle's horses. It's just that they won't insure her for the riskier ones," Jack explained. "It's mostly the scenes involving smoke and fire. That comes toward the end at the big climax of the movie. That's our deal — the wildfire sequences."

"Me and Diabolo — we're ready." Alisa sounded confident, but she was beginning to experience the first butterfly flutterings of the day.

"I know you'll be amazing — just like always," Kami insisted.

"You're feeling okay?" Jack asked Alisa as they came off the dirt road on to the highway and headed north.

She nodded. By now the sun was up and casting long shadows across the empty road. Another deer leaped a wire fence and ran in front of them, ears pricked and white tail bobbing. It quickly dashed off the highway.

"Then kick back and relax," he advised. "We have a long road ahead of us."

∾ ๏ ๏

Back at Stardust, the day got into full swing.

Tom finished feeding the horses and then went into the boys' dorm. He took a quick shower, got dressed, then flicked his towel across Zak's sleeping form. "Rise and shine," he cried to his rooming buddy.

"Uh-uh," Zak groaned. He turned over and buried his head under the covers. Rising and shining was not his strong point.

"Our turn to scoop poop in the corral," Tom reminded him. "Hayley, Becca, and Kellie are bringing the horses in from the meadow."

"Give me five more minutes."

"Sorry, bro, poop-scooping waits for no man!" After rubbing his towel over his super-short, light brown hair and running a toothbrush across his teeth, Tom returned to drag the blanket from Zak's bed.

"Hey, what did I ever do to you?" Zak moaned. He shivered as he slid into yesterday's clothes without showering.

"Gross," Tom commented.

Zak grunted and followed Tom out into the yard. "Why shower when you're shoveling horse manure?" he pointed out.

"I hear you." Whistling cheerfully, Tom strode into the tack room and grabbed two plastic shovels. He handed one to Zak, and together they went into the corral to start work.

Kellie glanced up at them from where Dylan was tethered. She'd already saddled her little dark bay Quarter Horse and was about to lead him into the round pen. "Hey, Tom, you were up early this morning," she teased.

"Was it to say goodbye to Kami?" Hayley added, bobbing up from behind Cool Kid.

"Uh," Tom grunted and then tried to deflect attention. "Say, Zak — how come you didn't get out of bed to wave goodbye to Alisa?"

"Sorry, bro — it won't work," Zak said. "We're on to you and Kami!"

◦

Tom decided it was best to keep his head down and not to take the bait. After he'd cleared the corral of horse droppings and Zak had driven the tractor out to the manure heap, he groomed Legend, his patient palomino mare.

"Guess what we're doing today," he mumbled into her ear after he'd looked around to check that the corral was empty. Talking to your horse and expecting an answer was not cool. "We're taking bareback lessons from Sheena Miller, who's only one of the best pro rodeo riders in the state."

Legend breathed out loudly through her nose.

Tom laughed. "Impressive, huh?" He looked around to see Lizzie emerge from the tack room without her usual broad smile. In fact, she was frowning.

"What happened? Did Sheena call to cancel?" he asked.

"No, no — it's nothing like that. Don't worry." Dressed in her trademark black shirt, Lizzie tried to brush off whatever it was that was worrying her. She started to groom Sugar, her sorrel mare, who was tied up in the corral beside Legend.

"It wasn't Jack on the phone, was it?" Tom double-checked. "They didn't have an accident with the trailer?"

"No, Tom. Relax — Kami and Alisa are fine." Sighing, Lizzie rested the currycomb on the rail where Sugar was tethered. "If you really want to know, it's my ex. You wouldn't believe what he's done now."

"Pete Mason? Let me guess." Tom knew that

Lizzie and Jack's rival was pitching hard for more stunt-riding contracts. "He's muscled his way into working on the *Wildfire* movie?"

"You got it," Lizzie said grimly. She took a deep breath. "I just found out that Mike Peterson chose a rider from there to work alongside Alisa and Diabolo in the action sequences."

"And?" Tom prompted.

"And the rider is Lucy Reeves, who we all know is very talented. I had no idea that she'd joined Pete's team for the summer. I tried to call Jack to warn him, but he didn't pick up."

"Maybe there's no signal."

"Yeah, maybe. I'll try again later."

"Wait, Lucy Reeves — as in Lucy Reeves, the junior national reining champion? Are you worried she'll outshine Alisa? There's no chance that'll happen," Tom insisted. "Alisa and Diabolo can hold their own in any company."

"Right," Lizzie muttered, apparently unconvinced. Then she paused and had second thoughts. "Actually, you are right. But that's not really the major problem. I also heard from Charlene Cross, my attorney in Colorado Springs, that Pete has hired a new big shot lawyer — a guy named Bradley Stewart. Charlene says they're about to make a fresh claim against Stardust."

"How can they do that?" Tom asked. "Didn't the divorce go through already?"

"Yeah, but not the financial settlement. Not according to Pete, anyway. He's insisting that he still has a stake in the outfit that Jack and I currently co-own." Lizzie paused to collect herself and to control the husky break in her voice. "To make a long story short, Pete Mason is claiming that half of the horses at Stardust still belong to him!"

Chapter 4

"So cool!" Kami hung out of the window as Jack drove the Stardust trailer into a parking lot just outside Estes Park.

Jack nodded. "You know how it is — when a film company is out on location, they take a whole mobile village along with them."

"Yeah, I remember from *Moonlight Dream*, but this is on a whole other level. There are so many trucks! Are the ones with the big awnings for the caterers?" Kami pointed to a row of trailers beneath some tall pinyon pines and Douglas firs.

"Yeah," Jack told her. "And these Jeeps in the parking lot belong to the crew."

Kami took in every detail, reminding herself of how she'd felt when she and Magic had arrived on the set of *Moonlight Dream*. It was cool to see the trailers and trucks all painted with their Diamond Studios logos. As soon as Jack had parked, she promised to get him a cup of coffee then scooted off to take a closer look around.

"Welcome," Rex Boyle said as he approached Alisa and Jack. "We're glad to have you here."

Alisa stood by as the two men shook hands. *They'll get along just fine*, she thought, noting that they shared the same tall, skinny physique and handsome, angular, weather-beaten features. And they seemed to respect one another from the get-go.

"I'd forgotten what a good-looking mount she is," Rex said as Jack unbolted the trailer door and Alisa stepped inside to fetch Diabolo. "You sure know how to pick out a nice-looking Quarter Horse."

"Actually, it was my wife," Jack explained. "Lizzie bought Diabolo long before I showed up."

"You hear that?" Alisa whispered in Diabolo's ear. "The head wrangler likes you. But don't let it go to your head!"

Diabolo shook out her shiny chestnut mane, soaking up the admiration.

"This is not a shampoo ad!" Alisa scolded. "Cut it out — we have work to do."

At that moment, Kami raced back with Jack's coffee and told Alisa all that she'd seen. "I just said hi to a bunch of actors standing outside the catering trailer. There was Scott Taylor, the kid who plays Joey in *Manhattan* — you know, the new soap. And the lady from the cop series set in Chicago . . ."

"Whoa, slow down," Alisa said as she led her high-stepping mare over to a nearby rail and tethered her.

"Sorry, I guess I'll have to get used to meeting famous people," Kami blushed, stepping aside as a dark-haired girl came over.

"Hey, you must be my stunt double," the girl said to Alisa.

It took a few seconds for Alisa to get her brain in gear. "Yeah, I'm Alisa Hamilton and this is my friend, Kami — she's part of the Stardust team. And y-you're Hannah?" she stammered. "Hannah Hart?"

"Yeah, sorry — I look different in the flesh." Hannah laughed. "Minus the lip gloss and the mascara, et cetera. You realize they do a ton of airbrushing on my publicity shots?"

"No, you don't . . . I mean, yeah." Alisa was babbling like an star-struck fan. *How many times have I done this?* she asked herself, blushing furiously. She wasn't a newbie like Kami — this was her third major contract for Stardust, not her first.

"So, anyway, introduce me to your horse," the A-list actress said. "What's your name, you drop-dead gorgeous creature?"

"Her name's Diabolo," Alisa said, trying to shake off her shyness. "This is our third summer working together."

"Wow, she's amazing." Hannah sighed.

"She is pretty perfect," admitted Alisa. Just as she knew Rex and Jack would get along, she felt she had an immediate bond with Hannah. "I hear you're doing some of your own stunts. Would you like to take a ride on Diabolo?" she asked.

"Really? You mean it?" Hannah's brown eyes shone.

"Sure. Just let me and Kami strap a saddle on." Alisa helped Kami lift the leather saddle from the rail and slide it on to Diabolo's back. She quickly ducked under the horse's belly and buckled the cinch. Meanwhile, Kami slipped the bridle between Diabolo's teeth.

"She's really friendly," Alisa told Hannah. "And gentle — honestly, she wouldn't hurt a fly."

In response to a friendly pat from Alisa, Diabolo arched her glossy neck and snorted. She waited patiently while Kami held the stirrup steady and the actress stepped into the saddle.

"Whoa, do we have insurance for this?" a guy from the technical crew called from the doorway of one of the trucks.

"Relax," Hannah told him. "I'm actually contracted to ride in this movie, and I'm not planning to take any risks here." She squeezed her legs against Diabolo's sides, and the mare turned away from the rows of trailers and stepped out under the tall, straight trees. "Let's try a trot," Hannah suggested, giving her a quick, light kick. Diabolo broke into a smooth trot. "And a lope," Hannah said.

"Jeez, watch the low branch!" the panicky crewmember yelled up the forested slope.

But there was no need to worry — Hannah was a confident rider, and Diabolo carried the valuable star wide of the branch, weaving easily in and out of trees toward a trail used by hikers and riders as a route to the top of the mountain.

Alisa and Kami followed on foot. When they caught up with Hannah, they found her already down on the ground, her arms wound lovingly around Diabolo's neck.

"So cool!" Hannah sighed happily. "I wish I had your job!"

"You totally don't," Alisa said with a smile. "Just think of the pay cut!"

"I wouldn't complain." Carefree in the middle of the forest, hair fanned out across her shoulders, Hannah admitted that the glamorous movie-star life had its downside. "Do you have any idea how long I spend in makeup every morning? And all those lines to learn, and the twenty-five takes to get a scene right. It drives me crazy." She handed Diabolo's reins to Alisa and stood back for one last admiring look. "Okay, so I sound like a spoiled brat."

"No, I get it. But tell her, Kami — she still wouldn't want to be a stunt rider: up before dawn, scooping poop, hosing down saddle blankets in the midday sun, not to mention the work we put in on the actual stunts . . ."

"I guess it's not easy falling off a horse without breaking multiple bones?" Hannah laughed.

"It takes practice," Kami assured her.

"Or riding through gunfire and cannons, past explosions, across raging rivers . . ."

"Through flames and smoke," Alisa added.

"Gee, yeah." Hannah stuck up her hands in surrender. "But I still do love Diabolo."

"We do, too," Alisa and Kami agreed enthusiastically.

∽ ◦ ℃

"So, no fire in this scene," Rex explained to Alisa as he walked her, Jack, and Kami through the first stunt. The director and the rest of the crew had left for lunch. Rex had taken the Stardust team up a mountain trail to a clearing bordered on the far side by an old-style, razor-wire fence designed to keep cows out of the park. In the clearing was a small wooden cabin.

Alisa had rolled up her sleeves and tied her hair in a high ponytail. She led Diabolo through the moves they would later make in front of the camera.

"This is the spot where Hannah's character gets shot. There's a killer hunkered down in the cabin as she rides by. He steps out with a rifle, shoots Hannah in the shoulder, and the horse in the neck — right here." Rex scuffed the dirt with the heel of his boot. "You recoil from the impact. At the same time, Diabolo rears up. You hang on to the saddle horn while your horse lands, then takes off toward that fence." Pointing across the clearing, Rex waited for Alisa to pace out the distance between him and the razor-wire barrier.

"They're going to make her and Diabolo jump the fence?" Kami asked Jack with a shiver. The blades twisted into the wires looked sharp and vicious.

Jack nodded. "Wait till you see them take off. It'll be spectacular."

"So, your horse doesn't stop," Rex instructed Alisa. "She heads straight for the fence and our hearts are in our mouths, but at the last second she jumps clean over."

Alisa nodded. "Is there much blood when I get shot?" she asked.

"Plenty. You and Diabolo will both be fitted with prosthetics. A rep from the Humane Association already checked it out and watched the special effects guys construct the plaster impression for the horse's wound. She'll be standing by on set to make sure we do everything properly. Do you want to try a dummy run?"

"No, we'll be fine," Alisa decided, her confidence building. After all, it was the kind of stunt she and Diabolo had spent their whole summers rehearsing back at Stardust Stables. "What time do we shoot the scene?"

"Three-thirty this afternoon."

She nodded then walked back across the grassy clearing to rejoin Kami and Jack. "I'm going to try to get this right the first time," she told them.

"Sounds good to me," Jack replied. Jack never had any doubts about Alisa's ability, but Kami was still trying to picture exactly how her friend would pull off the seemingly dangerous stunt.

"You all want to come and grab some lunch?" Rex asked, leading the way back through the trees.

Alisa shook her head. "Thanks, but no. You go ahead. I'm going to hand Diabolo over to the special effects department then get into costume and get fixed up ready to 'bleed'. Which shoulder do I get shot in?" she asked Rex.

"The right one."

"Cool." Walking her horse toward the costume trailer, she said goodbye to the others and carefully ran through the exact timing of the afternoon's stunt in her mind. "This is going to be fun," she told Diabolo. "I can't wait for Mr. Peterson to call 'Action!'"

∽ ◦ ℘

After lunch, Kami and Jack joined Alisa in the special effects tent as the technicians worked on Diabolo. Alisa explained to Kami the way the technical guys attached computer chips to the small bags of fake blood to make them burst at the press of a button and to look like authentic veins and arteries being shredded by bullets.

"Plus, of course, the guys fix a realistic prosthetic to Diabolo's neck — the side facing away from the first camera crew," Jack added.

He looked and sounded relaxed, leaning against the special effects trailer, thumbs hooked into his jeans pockets. "And you're all ready?" he checked with Alisa.

She nodded and pulled back her shirt to reveal the sachet of fake blood underneath.

"That's so neat!" Kami said.

"Good girl," Alisa murmured in Diabolo's ear as the team worked on.

"This is one patient animal," the woman who was fitting the prosthetic commented. "She's hardly moved a muscle the whole time I've been working."

Diabolo flicked her ears, as if she understood the praise.

"There — we're done," the technician said.

"You're Alisa Hamilton, Hannah's stunt double — right?" A runner came up, clipboard in hand. "We need you on set in five minutes."

Alisa nodded and, with one last check of her own sachet of fake blood, she said goodbye to Jack and Kami, then led Diabolo up the trail to the clearing where the action would take place.

"Relax," Jack advised a nervous Kami, who

nodded. "There's no need to feel like the third wheel here."

"I'm fine," Kami insisted as she set off with Jack up the hill. "Actually, I'm loving it."

Meanwhile, higher up the mountain, Rex checked a couple of things with Alisa.

"You're sure you don't want to rehearse this?"

"No, thanks." She was looking ahead toward a bunch of people gathered around a cameraman. Among them, she suddenly spotted the familiar face of Pete Mason! She gave a small groan as she recognized Lizzie's ex. "What's he doing here?" she mouthed over her shoulder at Jack.

Jack followed the direction of her gaze, stiffening when he saw Mason. He shrugged, then took out his cell phone and selected a number.

Meanwhile, Diabolo tossed her mane from her eyes and snorted. She was impatient to get to work.

Alisa looked again at the group of spectators and recognized a second person standing next to Mason — Lucy Reeves. "I haven't seen Lucy since I competed against her in Virginia," she muttered to herself.

Again Diabolo tugged at the reins. *Come on, let's go!*

Jack's going to be furious, Alisa thought. *And considering the way Pete's acted since the divorce from Lizzie, I'm not surprised.*

She, along with Kami, Hayley, Kellie, and the rest of the team back at Stardust, were one hundred percent convinced that Pete Mason had recently driven into Stardust Stables early one morning and opened the meadow gate to set the horses loose. It had been a mean trick, sabotaging newbie Kami just as she was about to set out for California on her first big contract.

And I'm not liking him any better now, Alisa thought darkly. Mason was heavyset, and his scowling face was fleshy and shadowed by a two-day stubble. He was wearing a denim shirt and a big fancy belt buckle, plus expensive-looking cowboy boots.

"Ready?" Rex's prompt jerked Alisa's attention back to the job. She had no more time to think about Mason and Lucy. A Jeep came up the trail and stopped to let Mike Peterson out.

The lighting and sound crews quickly took up their positions, followed by the actor playing the killer. As he stepped inside the old log cabin to wait for his cue, she heard Kami wish her luck as the director barked out instructions to the cameramen.

Meanwhile Jack approached Alisa for a final chat. "You're okay with everything?" he checked.

"Yeah. But what's Pete Mason doing here? And Lucy Reeves?"

"I have no clue. I just tried to call Lizzie, but I can't get a signal. We'll deal with it later. Let's just get on with the stunt."

Another runner sprinted up to Jack. "Mr. Peterson is ready to shoot now. Please step aside."

Taking a deep breath and vaulting into the saddle, Alisa cleared her head and focused on the stunt they had to perform. A guy with a clapperboard announced the scene number. The director called "Action!" She rode into the clearing in character, just like any normal, everyday girl without a care in the world.

"Easy," Alisa murmured to Diabolo, her whole body relaxing into the horse's steady walk. "Good girl, nice and easy."

Suddenly, as she and Diabolo reached the prearranged spot, the actor playing the killer flung open the cabin door, raised his repeat-action stunt rifle, and shot twice. *Bam! Bam!* Two loud cracks tore into the peaceful silence.

Instantly Alisa threw her weight way back in the saddle, dropped the reins, and twisted her torso, her left hand clutching her right shoulder.

The hidden sachet burst and crimson stained her white shirt. At the same moment the simulated gash on Diabolo's neck spurted with blood and she reared onto her hind legs.

Alisa grabbed the saddle horn with her left hand and allowed herself to be flung this way and that as Diabolo landed, put in a small buck for good measure, then took off toward the razor-wire fence.

Diabolo, you're such a diva! Alisa hid a smile as she lunged forward over the horn and her hair swung loose across her face. She maintained her balance, riding without reins so that it had to be Diabolo who judged her own pace and decided exactly when to take off. With her chestnut mane flying and wild eyes rolling, she left it to the last moment to jump the cruel barrier. Up and over.

"Cut!" Mr. Peterson called.

"Whoa!" Alisa murmured and Diabolo responded. She reached for the trailing reins and together they turned, re-took the fence at a steady lope, and arrived back in the clearing. "How was that?" she asked Rex, seeing that the director had already turned away to talk with one of his assistants.

With a big smile and a thumbs up, Rex gave the sign that the stunt had gone perfectly.

"No more takes?" Alisa asked. Her heart still pounded with leftover excitement.

"Nope, don't need 'em. The stunt was amazing. You got it right, first try," Rex told her. "See — even Mr. Peterson's happy."

Chapter 5

"If that was Mr. Peterson looking happy, I'd hate to see him when he's not," Alisa confided in Kami as she tethered Diabolo to the Stardust trailer and began to peel the flexible prosthetic wound from her neck.

"He's scary," Kami agreed. "But he's the director, so I guess it comes with the territory."

The fake blood had already dried into Diabolo's coat, so Alisa started to brush the dark red powder out. She was hard at work when Hannah briefly stopped by on her way to the costume trailer.

"Hey, beautiful girl!" she murmured, detouring to give Diabolo a gentle pat. "Here's hoping I get to ride you again soon."

"Any time," Alisa promised. She was pleased with their first day on set, but she grew uneasy when she saw Pete Mason deep in conversation with Lucy Reeves outside the catering tent. "Do we have any idea what he's doing here?" she asked Kami, who shook her head.

"Jack's been trying to call Lizzie to find out more, but he still can't get a signal."

When the girls saw Lucy break away from Mason and march toward them, their confusion grew worse.

"Hey, don't I know you?" Lucy began. She was a pretty girl with wavy dark hair, a round face, and even, white teeth. But her smile seemed forced as she began a conversation with her former rival.

Somehow the question made Kami bristle, but she tried not to show it.

"Alisa Hamilton," Alisa reminded Lucy, resting the brush against Diabolo's broad back.

"Ailsa . . . ?"

"Alisa," she repeated, separating out the syllables and speaking clearly.

"Alisa . . . ?" Lucy acted like she couldn't place her, but it was obviously fake. "Give me a clue."

"Virginia — last spring, the interstate reining competition."

"Oh, now I've got it! You were on a dark bay mare."

"Bonnie."

"Yeah, and I was on Sapphire. We beat you into second place."

Alisa smiled awkwardly and let Kami step in with a question. "Are you and Mr. Mason working on this movie, too?"

"Sure. Why else would we be here?"

"Who are you doubling for?"

"It's some C-list actor. I forget her name. Anyhow, she gets herself shot by the bad guy before he sets the forest on fire. They asked me to bring Sapphire along to perform a couple of special stunts." Edging Kami out of the conversation, Lucy turned her attention back to Alisa. "I see you're not riding your own horse."

"No, Bonnie's not trained to do film work. Besides, my mom and dad need her to work back home on the ranch."

"So, you figure you can build up the bond between you and this sorrel?" Lucy asked, arching an eyebrow and casting a doubtful eye over Diabolo. It was weird — she managed to make the word "sorrel" sound boring and third-rate. "Even when you only get to work together during the summer months?"

"You just saw what they did up there in the clearing," Kami butted in, dead set on sticking up for the Stardust duo. "So, yeah, I figure she can."

Lucy shrugged. "Pete likes it better if we train our own horses to do the stunts. And he's right. Sapphire is not only an interstate barrel-racing and reining champion, she's fabulous with vault tricks, one-foot drags, even back drags and spin the horn. There's nothing she can't do."

"I look forward to seeing her in action," Alisa said a little stiffly, deciding that getting back to grooming Diabolo was the best way to ease herself out of a conversation she wasn't enjoying.

There was an awkward silence for a moment, and then Rex appeared. "Let's walk through your first stunt," he told Lucy. "You and Sapphire will be doing a sideways drag with gunfire going on all around you, okay?"

"No problem," Lucy replied with that superior shrug that seemed to be her trademark.

Alisa and Kami watched them head up the mountain trail and breathed a sigh of relief now that Lucy was gone. They were even more pleased when Jack showed up and told them they were finished for the day.

"Alisa, walk Diabolo into the trailer. Kami, stash the tack in the cab. I'll try to call Lizzie again and let her know we'll be home early."

This time he got a signal, and he was busy on the phone while the girls set about their tasks. He was still talking as they finished loading Diabolo into the trailer.

"Problem?" Alisa asked.

He held up a hand. "Don't worry, Liz, it's not going to happen," he said. "You know Mason — he's just making empty threats."

There was silence for a moment while Lizzie responded, then another swift comment from Jack. "As a matter of fact, he's here on set with one of his stunt riders . . . Oh, you already knew that. Okay, no . . . I hear you."

The chopped, broken conversation made both Alisa and Kami worried.

"I promise I won't. No, I just want to speak with him . . . No, I won't get into an argument." He broke off with an abrupt "Bye" and slid his phone into his shirt pocket.

"Trouble?" Alisa asked as the normally calm and easy-going Jack paced back and forth.

"You won't believe the stupid trick Mason is trying to pull this time," he muttered. He forgot his promise to Lizzie and strode down the row of parked vehicles until he reached a silver horse trailer with the words "High Noon Stables" emblazoned in red-and-gold letters along the side. Seeing a figure sitting in the cab, he slammed his palm against the driver's door.

Kami and Alisa stood by anxiously as Pete Mason opened the door and stepped down. Watching the two men, they saw that Lizzie's ex was shorter than Jack, but heavier — and clearly angered by Jack's challenge.

"You touch my truck again and you're dead," he snarled.

"Lizzie just told me your latest game to try and beat us down," Jack shouted.

But Mason stopped him in his tracks by thrusting a broad palm against Jack's chest that sent him staggering back. "What's this got to do with you?" he yelled back.

Alisa ran across and tugged at Jack's arm. "Let's go," she urged. "We can't fix this by yelling, whatever it is."

Jack pulled away from Alisa, but her voice had gotten through to him. He took a long, deep breath then lowered his voice. "Seriously, no way are you going to win this one," he told Mason. "We're not going to roll over and let you take half the horses in our barn."

The words hit Alisa and Kami hard. So this was what had made Jack storm over to Pete Mason, and frankly, they didn't blame him.

"The Stardust business belongs to Lizzie," Jack insisted as Mason's face distorted into a nasty sneer. "She set it up all by herself while you wasted your time and her money on real estate deals that went bad the minute you touched them."

"Talk to my lawyer," Pete Mason jeered. "Bradley Stewart is confident I'm still owed half of what belongs to my ex-wife: namely, property and the stunt-riding business. And you can't do a thing about it."

"Not the horses," Jack insisted, his blood boiling again. "I'll make sure you don't lay a finger on them!"

Alisa and Kami saw him clench his fists and move in again toward Mason. This time it was Kami who came between them. "Jack, he's just winding you up," she insisted. "Let's go home and talk to Lizzie."

"Yeah, do what the pretty little lady tells you." Pete Mason laughed long and hard, only stopping when he saw one of Mr. Peterson's runners speed down the trail on a mountain bike.

"You have to come quick," he told Mason, braking hard and raising dirt. "Your girl didn't pull off the stunt for the gun-fight scene. Mr. Peterson is going nuts. He says he'll fire her unless you fix it quick."

Swearing, Mason turned and set off up the

hill without once looking back. Jack, Kami, and Alisa watched him disappear between the trees.

"Which horses does he want?" Kami asked. She felt her throat close up and her mouth go dry.

Jack shook his head. "Honestly, I don't know," he said through gritted teeth. The three of them walked back to their trailer, where Diabolo quietly munched hay from her net.

They climbed into the cab and Jack eased the trailer out of the parking lot. He turned onto the dirt road that would take them to the highway. Then they headed south without speaking, not even listening to the radio, each thinking their own uneasy thoughts.

No one noticed the spectacular, snowy peaks in the distance, nor the sun gradually sinking in the west.

Chapter 6

"I have a really bad feeling," Kami told Tom next morning.

It was their turn to bring the horses in from the pasture before anyone else was up, so they walked in the pre-dawn quiet by the side of Elk Creek, careful not to disturb the group of mule deer and their young taking a drink from the cool, clear water. The stag with his great, branching antlers stood higher up the slope, staring down warily at the human intruders.

"A bad feeling about Lucy Reeves?" Tom had already heard enough about Alisa's rival's rude behavior to understand that the problem was bound to get worse.

"Yeah, plus this other problem with Pete Mason. I've never seen Jack get angry like that before."

"I know. It hit Lizzie pretty hard, too."

"Did she say which horses he wants to get his hands on?" This was the unanswered question that had preyed on everyone's minds for the last twelve hours. It had meant that Kami had tossed and turned all night and gotten none of the sleep she needed. Luckily today, Monday, was a day off from filming. "I mean, I don't want any of the horses to leave Stardust — I don't even need to tell you that. And I know I've been here the shortest amount of time, but I really couldn't take it if Magic was on the list. Alisa feels the same way about Diabolo. It would break both our hearts."

Tom opened the meadow gate and then unhitched three halters from his shoulder. He waited for Legend to come trotting up. "I'd feel the same way if it was my girl," he agreed quietly.

For a while they said nothing, only breathing in the cool air and trying to see a way forward out of the present problem.

"Thanks, Tom," Kami said at last.

He smiled and reached for her hand. "For what?"

"For understanding what I'm saying. For being you."

"Hey," he murmured as he put an arm around her shoulder.

She smiled up at him, but then Legend chose that exact moment to come up and nuzzle hungrily at Tom's pockets, making them step apart.

He laughed and pushed her away. "Don't be so greedy!"

Kami smiled. "She's only looking for treats."

"No treats for you today," Tom told Legend.

Meanwhile Magic had ambled up to Kami to say hi.

"Hey, boy," she murmured, gently easing a halter into place and lifting Magic's dark gray forelock out of his eyes. "I missed you yesterday, but today we get to work in the arena together."

"So, back to the big issue," Tom reminded Kami as he rounded up Legend, Cool Kid, and Sugar, then started the trek back to the corral. "The way I hear it, Pete Mason hasn't given Lizzie an actual list."

Kami followed with Diabolo, Dylan, and Magic. Their hooves swished through the long grass, and she felt their warm breath on her neck and shoulders. "I know, but this is stress that we don't need, and it's going to get worse before it gets better," she predicted as they used the rickety wooden footbridge to cross the creek.

"I guess there's nothing we can do about it

right now, so let's not think any more about Pete Mason," Tom decided. "We shut the problem out of our heads, work hard, and have fun."

∞ ◦ ∞

"This is what I love!" Kami told Lizzie. She and Magic had just finished a complicated combination of vaults and shoulder stands followed by a front wing, all rounded off with a spectacular saddle fall. They had arrived in the center of the round pen for Lizzie's expert verdict. "It's so cool when this stuff works — I never want to do anything else."

"Nothing scares that girl," Kellie told her brother, Tom, as they waited in the corral on Dylan and Legend. "She has the guts to pull off any stunt Lizzie asks her to do. Soon she'll be up there with Alisa, competing for the top jobs."

Tom nodded, then couldn't help blushing as his sister leaned sideways and nudged him with her elbow.

"She's cute, too, huh?" Kellie kidded.

Tom said nothing. He smiled, remembering his early morning walk to the meadow with Kami and the moment when he put his arm around her shoulder.

Meanwhile, Hayley and Alisa drove two yearling Hereford calves out of the barn and across the corral toward the gate into the round pen. The girls were on foot and brandishing long willow sticks, but they were having trouble guiding the wayward cows.

"Yip!" Hayley cried. "Yip, girls, yip!"

Without warning, the yearlings split apart and made skittish runs in different directions. Kellie and Tom launched Dylan and Legend into action, chasing the brown and white calves around the corral, cornering them, then turning them back toward the round pen.

"Come on in, everyone," Lizzie called. "Drive those calves in here with you. They belong to Jason Donohue up at High Ridge Ranch, but I brought them in especially for you, Kellie. I want you to get Dylan ready to learn some new moves for your Texas job."

"Cutting and roping," Tom explained to Kami. "Dylan's a real cow horse; he was born to round up cattle. You'll see — it's a blast!"

"Becca and Alisa, I want you and your horses to drive the calves across the center of the pen nice and slow." Lizzie was mounted on Sugar, issuing instructions to each rider in turn. "Zak, come and join us. You two boys will cut across in front of them at a flat gallop. The idea is that the cows will have to suddenly switch direction. Kami and Hayley, your job is to lope full circle around the rim of the arena, yee-hahing and messing things up for Kellie. Kellie, you drive these runaway Herefords into a tight spot where you can lean out and rope them in one at a time. Everybody got that?"

"Yeah, we're ready," Becca replied. "Come on, Alisa. Let's get these critters moving."

The stunt needed complete concentration, but there was an easy, relaxed mood among the young riders as they got the chance to work together as a team.

"These calves have no clue what we want them to do," Tom told Kami before she and Hayley set out around the perimeter. "Remember, they're not smart like horses. All they want to do is cut and run."

"Hmm, actually that seems pretty smart to me," Kami commented. She knew that if she was a cow being rounded up for market, cutting and running was exactly what she would want to do.

"Yip!" Alisa cried, setting off from the gate and letting Diabolo nudge the calves forward.

"Ready, Tom? Ready, Zak?" Lizzie called. "Now go!"

The two boys dug their heels into their horses' sides, then galloped across the round pen. They skidded to a halt within inches of the high wooden fence.

"Whoa!" Hayley cried out as the calves lurched to their left to avoid Legend and Ziggy. "Over to you, Kellie!"

Kellie charged after the runaways, lasso in hand. She leaned out of the saddle, raised the coiled rope above her head, aimed, and threw. She held her breath as the rope snaked through the air, but the calf lurched suddenly and lunged off in a new direction. The rope landed in the dirt.

"Jeez, sorry!" Kellie groaned and started to gather in the rope.

"Again," Lizzie called. "Don't worry, Kellie. Let's start the whole thing over."

∾ ⊙ ℘

"I told Lizzie earlier, I just love this job!" Kami confessed to Alisa as they watered their horses in the big metal trough by the corral gate.

"I love it as much as you do," Alisa agreed. "I don't ever want to do anything else."

"Maybe we won't have to," Kami said.

The two girls were enjoying spending more and more time together. Once they had watered their horses and tethered them in the shade, they took bagged lunches out to the creek. They sat on a smooth rock with their bare feet dangling. "Here's hoping we can make a career out of stunt riding and do it for the rest of our lives."

"That would be cool." Munching her peanut butter and jelly sandwich, Alisa was trying hard to forget the problems of yesterday. Now she sat with Kami and enjoyed the sunny moment. "Would you like half my sandwich?"

"No, thanks. How can you eat that junk?" Kami asked.

"What do you mean — whole wheat bread is good for me!" Alisa laughed. Besides, the peanut butter and strawberry jelly mix had been her favorite since forever.

Suddenly Kami heard horses approaching. They were coming fast, splashing and clattering their hooves on the rocky bed. "Uh-oh, watch out!" Kami warned. She leaped to her feet ahead of Alisa, who was still biting into her sandwich.

"Go, Zig!" Zak called as he came into view. His horse loped and created a huge splash as he surged knee-deep through the water. Tom and Legend showed up soon after.

"Quick, Alisa, they plan on drowning us!" Kami scrambled to safety farther up the steep bank.

"Stop!" Alisa yelled to attract the boys' attention.

"It's no use! They're doing it on purpose . . ." Kami's voice faded. It was too late.

"Hey!" Alisa shrieked. She jumped up and let her hat fall from her lap into the creek. Tom and Zak loped by. Ice-cold creek water showered the girls and drenched them from head to foot.

"Whoops!" Tom laughed as they rushed by.

"Traitor!" Kami cried. "Tom, I thought you were my friend!"

"He is," Alisa insisted as she slid back down the bank to fish out her Stetson.

"Then why did he do that?" Kami watched Alisa retrieve the soggy hat and tip the water out.

"Because he's your 'friend'."

"But that's so dumb." Kami stared in dismay at her wet shirt and jeans.

"That's what they do." Alisa sighed. "I've worked with these guys for two years, so I should know."

∽ ◉ ઝ

"Dude, that was a blast!" Tom reined Legend back and trotted her up the bank and onto the Jeep track leading back to Stardust.

"Did you see Alisa?" Zak called over his shoulder. "We were right on target. She couldn't have been more wet if we'd thrown her in the pool!"

Tom leaned forward to pat and reassure Legend. "Those girls will be so mad," he warned. "They're going to want to get back at us."

"We'll be ready," Zak said.

"We will?" Tom said with a sigh. He was beginning to feel uneasy about the trick they'd played. "Why did I agree to do that?"

"Chill out," Zak advised. "You're just worried Kami won't looove you anymore!" he kidded, weaving Ziggy between the tall trees that lined the dirt track.

"I'm serious." Raising his hat, Tom ran a hand through his stubbly hair. "She's new here, and she might not get our oddball humor."

Zak nodded, then grew more thoughtful. "How's she doing with Alisa up in Estes Park?"

"Good. Jack says the girls make a great team." There was a pause as the boys glanced down and spotted Alisa and Kami taking a short cut with their horses along the side of the creek.

"You know they were there when it all kicked off between Jack and Pete Mason?"

"When Jack heard the 'rumor'." Zak made air quotes with his fingers.

"It's more than a rumor. Pete Mason definitely wants half our horses — I heard it straight from Lizzie."

"He can take a hike." Zak shook his head. "I mean, no way will we let him."

"Lizzie was planning to drive into town to meet with her attorney, Charlene Cross. She should be there right now. They're talking through the latest development."

"Which is?"

"Lizzie has Mason's actual list."

"Of horses' names?" This part was news to Zak. Although rumors spread rapidly among members of the Stardust team, he hadn't realized that things had progressed this far. "Says who?"

"Becca," Tom told him, still watching Alisa and Kami as they went through the willows bordering the meadow. "She was in the tack room just before lunch. She swears she saw the names scrawled on a piece of paper by the phone. It was Lizzie's handwriting. There were six horses."

"Whoa!" Zak halted Ziggy. "Why didn't you tell me?"

"Because it came from Becca," Tom pointed out. "I guess I was hoping she'd made it up."

"And if she didn't . . . ?"

"You want to know who was actually on the list?"

Zak nodded and swallowed hard. "Was Ziggy there?"

"No. And neither was Legend." Tom almost felt guilty that his own horse wasn't included.

"So, who?"

Slowly Tom named names. "Jack's horse, Liberty, and Lizzie's, Sugar. They're warmbloods, so they're the most valuable horses in the stable."

"No way!" Zak said. "Who else?"

"Kami's Magic and Hayley's Cool Kid."

Zak pictured the tears and heartbreak. He turned his face up toward the mountain to hide his own emotions. "And?"

"Pepper and Diabolo," Tom muttered. "I had to grab a hold of Becca and tell her no way should she mention it to Alisa. I said it could be any old list that Lizzie had made — horses needing new shoes, extra feed, whatever."

"I guess." Zak didn't really believe this, though. Liberty, Sugar, Magic, Cool Kid, Pepper, and Diabolo — Pete Mason would be the first to recognize that these were among the best stunt horses in the business. "Did Becca agree not to tell Alisa?"

"Yep," Tom said quietly, walking Legend on down the track. The sun was hot on his back, but it didn't relax him — he was too wound up for that. "I told her how important it was for Alisa to focus on the *Wildfire* job and not get freaked out over Mason's mean moves. I really laid it on the line."

"Yeah, well, let's hope she listened," Zak murmured.

But Becca was Becca. Both Tom and Zak knew that of all the riders at Stardust, she was the one they trusted the least.

Chapter 7

It was with a heavy heart that Kami slipped out early the next morning to visit Magic in the meadow. The previous night she'd run into Becca on the tack-room porch and they'd had the worst conversation of their lives — so bad that Kami could still hardly believe it was true.

"No way!" she'd gasped. She felt like she had been punched in the stomach.

Holding back her emotions, Becca had repeated the names on Mason's list. "Sugar and Liberty, Cool Kid and Pepper, Diabolo and Magic."

"No — not Magic!" Kami had protested. "Not my beautiful boy!"

"Pepper, too," Becca had said, choking up.

They'd stared at each other in the gathering dusk, their eyes filled with tears.

Now, pre-dawn and after another sleepless

night, Kami realized that no one else was up —
not even Alisa, who was due on set in Estes Park
by mid-morning.

"Hey," Kami sighed when Magic trotted up
to her as she stood by the gate. She reached out
to stroke his dappled neck and run her fingers
through his dark forelock.

Magic nudged her shoulder with his nose.
What's up?

"Nothing. Everything's cool," she insisted.

He nudged her again, as if he didn't believe
her.

Kami put her arms around his neck. "If you
must know, you're on Pete Mason's list," she
confided. "Becca gave me six names — you were
one of them." Even just telling Magic that they
might have to part brought more tears to her eyes.
"I won't let him do it," she vowed, though she had
no idea how she would keep her promise. "We're
a team, you and me. They'll never trailer you out
to High Noon, whatever the lawyers decide."

Magic took a step back and tilted his head to
one side as if considering what she'd just said.
Then he pricked his ears in the direction of the
corral, picking up a sound. Sure enough, Alisa
came out on to the tack-room porch carrying
Diabolo's halter.

"And we're not going to tell Alisa," Kami went on, fighting back her tears. "Diabolo's on the list too, but Zak, Tom, and I, we all made Becca swear to keep it from her."

Magic dipped his head as if agreeing.

"Good boy," Kami murmured, putting on a brave face and stepping forward to greet Alisa.

"Hey, Kami! It's a beautiful day." Alisa looked up to where the sun was rising in the east. "You're coming along for the ride again?"

Kami grinned. "Not even wild horses could stop me."

"Cool. You know who else is up and having breakfast?"

Kami took a guess. "Tom?"

"You wish!" Alisa grinned. "Actually, no. It's Becca. I just ate with her."

Kami let out a gasp. If Becca had broken her promise to keep Pete Mason's list secret, she thought she might just have to kill her. But then, Alisa didn't seem overly upset.

"Miracles do happen. She was actually . . ." Alisa fished for the right word. ". . . friendly!"

"Wow."

"I know. She wished me luck for today's stunts."

"Wow, again." Swiftly Kami moved on.

"Listen, I asked Jack and he said we could bring Magic with us today. He'll keep Diabolo company in the trailer, and then he and I can ride out and explore the area while you two are working."

It seemed like a good plan, so the two girls put halters on their horses and walked them through the dewy meadow, across the bridge, and into the corral.

Before long they'd laid straw in the trailer and loaded the tack, brushed down Magic and Diabolo, and were ready and waiting for their driver.

"Jack's just finishing his eggs and bacon," Becca called from the ranch-house porch. "He'll be with you in a couple of minutes."

"You're right," Kami commented as they watched Becca cross the yard and talk to Tom and Zak outside the boys' dorm. "She's being nice for a change."

"And why is she awake right now? Why is she talking to Zak and Tom this early in the morning?" Alisa paused for thought. "I bet it's this problem with Pete Mason."

"Let's not waste time guessing. Come on, let's load the horses." Again Kami was eager to change the subject. "Magic first, then you can follow with Diabolo."

They'd hardly finished when they saw Becca split away from the boys and head for the trailer.

Uh-oh. Kami held her breath. *Please, Becca — don't spread rumors until we know they're true!*

"More news about Pete Mason!" Becca announced, looking serious. "You want me to fill you in on the latest?"

"No!" Kami shot out her answer, getting a confused look from Alisa.

"Don't worry, this is good news," Becca assured her. With her blond hair tied back in a high ponytail and wearing a similar dark blue T-shirt to Kami's, it was hard to tell the two girls apart. "Late last night I called my dad."

"And?"

"He's a big-shot divorce lawyer in Denver," Becca explained. "I told him what the deal was with Pete Mason and Bradley Stewart, and he said they'd need written proof that Mason is entitled to any part of Lizzie's business: a proper signed contract."

"And do we know he doesn't have one?" Alisa asked.

"Not yet. But my dad also said he'd visit Stardust and look through all the papers with Charlene Cross and together they would talk to Lizzie about the case. So that's great."

"Yeah, that is good news," Kami and Alisa agreed.

"Dad's cool — he understands that I'd hate to lose Pepper." As she was speaking, Becca choked up and had to turn away.

Alisa frowned. This was so unlike the usual brash and confident Becca. "Has Mason said that Pepper is one of the horses he wants?"

Don't say a word! Kami thought, fidgeting at Alisa's side and wishing with all her might that Jack would hurry up.

Becca turned back to face them. "No," she said quietly, catching Kami's eye. "I'm just saying 'if' — if he turned out to be on Mason's list."

"That's how we all feel," Alisa assured her, and she went into the trailer to check on Magic and Diabolo one last time.

Kami gave a sigh of relief. "Thanks!" she mouthed at Becca as the ranch door opened and Jack finally came out.

∽ ◦ ഛ

Up in Estes Park, on the *Wildfire* set, there was plenty of action. Jack asked Kami and Alisa to unload the horses while he went to find Rex and run through the day's stunts.

"Has anybody seen Rex?" Jude Amery, a young assistant director, hurried out of the special effects trailer and approached the girls as they tethered Diabolo and Magic to a rail.

"No, but Jack went to find him," Alisa replied.

Meanwhile, makeup and wardrobe assistants scurried between their own departments. Scott Taylor, the kid from the *Manhattan* series, and a bunch of extras hung around outside the catering tent, drinking coffee.

Scott overheard the conversation. "Rex is with Pete Mason," he told the assistant director. "There may be another issue with Lucy's horse."

"Wrong, wrong!" Lucy, too, had overheard and issued the denial at full volume from the High Noon trailer. She put on her dazzling smile when she spotted Kami and Alisa tacking up Magic and Diabolo. She strode straight across. "Pete and Rex are chilling together over a cup of coffee, that's all. What's with the gray horse?" she asked abruptly. "Did Rex hire him as an extra?"

Kami shook her head. "Magic is Diabolo's best buddy. He came along for the ride, the way I did."

Alisa felt they didn't owe Lucy any lengthy explanations. "So, how did you and Sapphire get along in the shoot-out scene?"

"We got it in three takes," Lucy replied stiffly. "Boy, these movie guys are so ignorant. They don't realize that a horse is not a machine — that they're going to react to stuff. It took Pete an age to explain that a cameraman can't just stick his lens in Sapphire's face, that horses are going to spook big time if you do that to them."

Alisa clicked her tongue, either in agreement or disagreement. It was hard to tell.

"Next time Pete will personally work out the stunts in advance and have every detail written into our contract. He knows way more than Rex Boyle ever will when it comes to staging gunfights and stuff."

"Watch out — here he comes now." Kami warned Lucy to lower her voice. Then she offered to take care of Diabolo while Alisa and Rex ran through the day's stunts.

Rex gave no sign that he'd overheard Lucy's last remark. He just tipped the rim of his Stetson in greeting and told Kami that Jack was in the catering tent if she wanted to catch up with him there. Then he nodded to Alisa to follow him.

"So, you're new to Stardust?" Lucy leaned against the Stardust trailer, talking to Kami in the same know-it-all tone. "You weren't there when Pete ran the place?"

"I don't think he ever ran things," Kami protested, stooping to finish tightening Diabolo's cinch.

"I guess morale's pretty low right now, since Pete set up High Noon in competition."

"Morale's fine, thanks."

"Let me check that," Lucy offered, almost pushing Kami aside and jerking at the thick leather girth strap. "It needs to go up a notch or two. And you see this latigo? This slots through here like this."

Luckily Hannah showed up just as Kami reached her boiling point.

"Hey, how's my favorite girl?" The actress practically glowed as she stroked Diabolo. She asked Kami if it was okay to give her a bite of apple.

"Sure, go ahead," Kami told her, trying not to be overawed. Hannah was everything that Alisa was, and then some. Her hair was glossier, her brown eyes bigger. She was so slim and elegant in her Wrangler jeans and Cuban-heeled boots.

"I have half an hour to spare before they need me for my next scene," Hannah told Kami. "Do you think Alisa would mind if I rode Diabolo again?"

"Hey, you're the star," Lucy reminded her

as she stepped in between them and offered Hannah a leg up. "You don't even have to ask."

Hannah's smile was radiant as she eased herself into the saddle. "You want to ride with me?" she asked Kami.

Did she want to?! In a flash, and deliberately ignoring Lucy's sullen glance, Kami was mounted on Magic and ready to accompany the star. She hardly noticed that Lucy was now fussing over Diabolo's tack.

"You're good to go," Lucy told Hannah at last. "You take care now."

"We won't go far," Hannah called over her shoulder. "Just up the forest trail a little ways."

∽ ◦ ∾

Meanwhile, as Rex and Alisa walked up the mountain, Alisa got familiar with the details of her next stunt.

"This is the reason Mr. Peterson hired you," Rex reminded her. "He liked what he saw in the round pen at Stardust Stables — you expertly riding your horse through the flaming arches. It was very impressive. But now you have to really prove yourself. Now you have to deal with the real thing."

"So you're really going to set the forest on fire?" Alisa asked.

"That's how it'll look," he explained. "But we're at nine thousand feet and you see up there, above the tree line?"

Alisa nodded. Ahead of them the aspens thinned out until eventually there was bare rock.

"That's where we're filming, with the wind coming up the mountain from the southwest, fanning the flames toward the bare peak. We'll set up a fake screen of burning trees and film you and your horse galloping through the flames."

"Cool." Alisa didn't say much — she was concentrating hard and taking in every aspect of her surroundings.

"Here's the back story for this part of the plot: the area has had no rainfall all summer, and the U.S. Forest Service has set up a red alert. So our resident psycho decides to set a controlled fire on the outskirts of town, then act the hero by saving Hannah's character from the flames. Only, the wind changes direction and he sets the whole forest on fire."

"So Hannah's character grabs her horse and tries to escape?" Alisa guessed.

"Right. The helicopters are already on the scene, dousing the flames from above. A team of firefighters ropes in to contain the fire. It's high-octane action — flames, water, guys dropping from choppers on ropes, and just you and your horse racing to outrun the inferno."

"Expensive," Alisa murmured. All those helicopters and stuntmen dropping from the sky, all those gallons of water and hissing flames and churning chopper blades.

"Very." Rex stopped and stood looking closely at Alisa, thumbs hitched into his belt. "Your part of the filming's going pretty well so far. Let's hope today goes smoothly, too, since we really need to do this in one take."

"Diabolo and I will do our best," she promised. She'd already staked out the territory and seen exactly how hard the riding would be. But she felt confident that it was nothing she and Diabolo couldn't handle.

The head wrangler gave a small, satisfied nod. "So this is where we position the screen of burning trees," he explained, walking on. "From this pillar-shaped boulder on your left to the clump of round rocks to the right, about ninety feet away. Got it?"

Alisa nodded and stored the information.

"And that's where you race your horse up the mountain, following the trail toward the bare ridge with sheer cliffs to either side. We'll have cameras filming from every angle. Your job is to ignore the choppers and the firefighters. Just ride like crazy through the smoke to safety."

Chapter 8

"So Kami, I heard you stunt-doubled for Coreen Kessler in *Moonlight Dream*?" Hannah chatted easily as she rode Diabolo up the forest trail away from the trailers and tents.

"It was my first job for Stardust," Kami told her. "We shot the scenes on the beach in southern California. They chose Magic and me because Magic likes to swim. He's so good around water."

"The same way Diabolo is good with fire?"

"Yes. Each horse on the string has a specialty." Though she was modest about her own ability, Kami didn't hold back when it came to praising the Stardust equines. "With Dylan, it's cows. He's a natural around them. Plus, he can play dead better than anyone else," she said. "He gets it right every time."

"You mean he just drops down and lies there without moving a muscle?" Laughing at the idea, Hannah rode a little way ahead. "Sounds like this Dylan is a great actor — better than some A-listers I've come across!"

There was more laughter between the girls as they stopped in the shade of some pinyon pines. Noticing that Magic had pricked his ears and turned his head back down the slope, Kami glanced over her shoulder to see that Lucy Reeves was following them on Sapphire. The rangy Appaloosa was picking her way across a stretch of bare rock, sliding a little on the smooth surface as Lucy urged her on.

"Should we wait for her?" Kami asked Hannah uncertainly.

Looking at her watch, Hannah shook her head. "I only have thirty minutes before they need me for my next scene. What do you say we try a lope up that sandy draw?"

"Go ahead," Kami invited, watching Hannah squeeze Diabolo's sides. Alisa's sorrel launched herself into an easy canter. "But watch out for hidden ditches and wash-outs."

"Yee-hah!" Giving a high-spirited cowboy yell, Hannah asked Diabolo for more speed and the brave sorrel responded, even though the loose surface made the going tough.

Kami clicked her tongue and Magic followed. Soon he was right on Diabolo's heels.

But then suddenly Kami grew concerned. There was something wrong with Diabolo's saddle — the latigo was flapping free and the whole saddle was slipping to the right-hand side.

"Ease up!" Kami yelled, as Magic strained to overtake Diabolo. She waved her arm to attract Hannah's attention and tried to point at Diabolo's loosening cinch. But Hannah had the wind in her ears and she was facing straight ahead, grinning and thinking that they were in a race.

"Whoa!" Kami cried as Hannah's girth strap flew loose and the saddle slid sideways.

Hannah felt it go. At the last moment she tried to right herself by putting all her weight into her left stirrup as Diabolo galloped on. It was too late — the saddle slid from Diabolo's back and Hannah fell with it.

Within seconds Kami brought Magic to a halt and vaulted from the saddle. She knelt beside Hannah, who lay on her back, eyes closed.

Kami's heart shuddered and missed several beats. There were sharp rocks all around, half hidden by sand. She prayed that Hannah hadn't struck her head on one. She gently swept the star's hair from her face. "Please wake up," she murmured.

More hooves pounded up the slope and soon

Lucy and Sapphire arrived. "What were you thinking?" Lucy yelled at Kami, who glanced up with frightened tears in her eyes. "How could you even think of letting Hannah lope up this wash-out?"

"It was the saddle," Kami mumbled. Her head was spinning. What if Hannah was badly hurt? She blamed herself for agreeing to the ride — she who knew horses inside out, who should have taken better care of her companion. "The cinch came loose," she explained.

"Wait here," Lucy snapped, reining Sapphire around to point downhill. "Don't try to move her. I'll get help."

As Kami waited beside Hannah, Diabolo and Magic stood with heads hanging in the shade of a tall rock. Diabolo's saddle lay in the dust nearby. Hannah's face was pale. There was sand on her forehead and cheek, but no visible cuts. As Kami watched, Hannah's eyelids began to flicker, and at last she opened her eyes.

"Where am I?" Hannah's voice was slurred at first and her eyelids drooped.

"It's okay," Kami told her. "Lucy has gone to get help. Lie still, please!"

But Hannah struggled to raise her head. "What happened? Did I fall off my horse?"

"Your saddle slipped. How are you feeling?"

"I'm good," Hannah said groggily as she raised herself onto her elbows. Then she tried a joke. "I guess I should learn to fall off a horse safely, the way you stunt guys do it."

"Please, don't get up. You might have broken something. We should wait for a medic." Still panicking, Kami pleaded with Hannah to lie down again.

"No, I can move — watch me." Gingerly Hannah picked herself up. "Ouch!"

"What hurts?" Kami gasped.

"My head, my ribs, everything. But I'm okay, really."

Just then Kami heard voices. Moments later Rex and Alisa, along with Lucy and a female paramedic carrying a backpack, appeared.

As soon as the paramedic saw Hannah trying to walk, she broke into a run. Behind them, Kami spotted a Jeep with Jude Amery, the assistant director, at the wheel and — worst of all — Mike Peterson in the passenger seat!

The paramedic guided Hannah to the nearest flat rock and began running through a checklist: first the patient's pulse, then her vision, followed by ease of movement in all her joints. Meanwhile, Kami hurried to meet Alisa and Rex.

"What happened? Is she okay?" Alisa was the first to speak.

As Kami nodded, her tears spilled over and rolled down her cheeks. "She wanted to lope. I should've stopped her."

"No, you couldn't have known there'd be an accident," Alisa countered. "Hannah is a good rider."

"So why is the saddle lying in the dirt?" Rex got straight to the point. "Did the cinch break?"

"It came loose," Kami confessed.

The head wrangler raised an eyebrow, but he said nothing. He stepped aside to allow Mr. Peterson through. The director's expression was dark as he checked on the medical status of his star.

"Who is the idiot is responsible for this?" he yelled after a quick and presumably reassuring talk with the paramedic. He turned on Alisa and Kami, with Lucy hanging back behind the Jeep. "Who thought letting Hannah ride a stunt horse was a good idea?"

"Me," Hannah called weakly from her rock. "It was my idea. I asked if I could ride Diabolo. It's all my fault."

But Mr. Peterson ignored her. "Are you dumb?" he yelled at Alisa and Kami. Suddenly he spotted

Jack running up the hill. "Hey, Jones! This is down to you! You let these kids fool around on the horses when your back was turned!"

Jack quickly took in the scene, his mouth set in a thin, grim line. "Alisa, Kami — go fetch the horses," he muttered without looking at either of them. Then he strode over and lifted Diabolo's saddle out of the dirt. "It won't happen again," he assured the angry director.

"You bet your life it won't," Mr. Peterson stormed. For a moment it looked as if he was about to fire the whole Stardust team on the spot, then Rex stepped in for a quiet word.

"Fire . . . big scene . . . all set to go," the wrangler reminded the director in a low voice.

Mr. Peterson mumbled a few angry words then took a deep breath, all the while staring at Alisa as she went up to Diabolo and gathered her reins.

"No other horse . . . no other rider is capable," Rex insisted quietly.

Still Alisa and Kami waited for the axe to fall.

Mr. Peterson grunted, then walked back to the Jeep. As he passed Jack, who was standing with his hands on hips and the brim of his hat pulled low over his forehead, he slowed down. "If there was any other horse and rider who could perform this stunt, you'd be out right here, right now," the director warned. "So tell your girl there are no second chances. She shows up on set later today. Either she gets her scene right on the first take, or I throw you, her and her horse, and the whole damned Stardust outfit off the movie — out of the whole stunt-riding world — for good!"

∿ ⊙ ℅

"But Hannah adores Diabolo! It was her idea. She wanted to ride her!" Kami repeated the same phrases to anyone who would listen as she and Alisa tethered Magic and Diabolo to the rail next to their trailer. They headed for the catering tent, which was busy with members of the crew.

"Even so . . ." Jude Amery's shrug conveyed a thousand words. No way should a valuable star like Hannah Hart be riding a stunt horse.

"Yeah, well . . ." A woman from special effects couldn't think of anything reassuring to say. So she, too, gave a shrug and wandered off.

"It was me — I told her she could ride Diabolo any time she wanted," Alisa insisted. "So Mr. Peterson can't blame Kami!"

"Lucky for you, Hannah didn't get seriously injured," Lucy commented. She'd come down from the mountain in the director's Jeep, then taken her time walking over to the catering tent. "Lucky again that she's telling everyone it was an accident, pure and simple."

Jude quickly picked up on this. "Which you obviously don't think it was?"

It was Lucy's turn to give the non-committal shrug. "Cinches don't come loose, and saddles don't just slip off by accident," was all she said before she poured herself some coffee. "That only happens when someone's been careless."

It was a killer line, delivered in Lucy's typical sneering tone. It left an uncomfortable silence around the table as she stalked off back to the High Noon trailer.

"Ouch." A girl from makeup gave a grimace, then left her seat.

Pretty soon everyone had faded away, leaving Alisa and Kami alone in the catering tent.

"This is definitely not our best day ever," Alisa said with a sigh, underplaying events to make Kami feel better. "Don't you wish we could rewind and start over?"

Kami nodded and took a long cool drink of soda. At last her heart was slowing down to its normal pace, and her head had almost stopped spinning. "Alisa, I'm so sorry . . . " she began.

"Me, too. I never came across this situation before, where the star of the movie wants to ride my horse. Most actresses are too fixated on their makeup and hair to risk getting messy on horseback."

"You couldn't have known this would happen," Kami insisted. "You weren't even there."

"Right. But I didn't stop to think it through when Hannah first asked if she could ride Diabolo. And the worst thing is, I let Jack down. It's not as if he and Lizzie don't have enough to deal with right now — Pete Mason and lawyers, all the worries about losing half our horses." Alisa sighed. "We'll just have to make the best of it. I'm needed on set pretty soon. As for you — try to forget about what happened to Hannah, okay? Take good care of Magic and make sure he has plenty of water to drink. I'll see you later."

"No, Alisa, wait!" Suddenly Kami stood up and followed her out of the tent. "You heard what Lucy said. Cinches don't come loose, and saddles don't fall off by accident."

"That's just Lucy being mean. Don't listen to her."

"Actually, she's right." It was as if a mist had cleared inside Kami's head and she remembered in detail what had happened. "But not in the way she wants everyone to believe. Think about it — there's got to be a reason why Diabolo's latigo came loose and the buckle on the cinch slipped. And I swear to you, it wasn't me being careless."

"What are you saying?" Alisa stopped mid-stride.

"You know me — I'd never do that."

"So, who fastened the cinch?" Alisa asked slowly.

"I did," Kami remembered. "Then Lucy stepped in to tighten it."

"Let me check that," Lucy had offered, and Kami recalled it now word for word. And she saw again in her mind's eye how Lucy had spent ages adjusting the strap and slotting the latigo into place. Then Lucy had stepped back to fiddle with the tack again, once Hannah had mounted Diabolo. That was the moment, Kami realized now, when Lucy had come up with her dirty trick.

"What are you saying?" Alisa asked again, feeling her stomach tighten into a knot. "That Hannah's fall was no accident?"

Kami nodded. "Lucy set it up to make it look like it was our fault," she insisted. "She didn't tighten the cinch — she loosened it!"

Chapter 9

"Without proof, what are we going to do?" Jack said, after Kami and Alisa finished sharing their thoughts about the loose cinch.

"But Lucy set us up," Kami protested. "She's jealous. She wanted something bad to happen so Alisa and Stardust would take the blame."

"And I'm certain Pete Mason is happy it happened," Alisa went on. "He enjoys anything that harms our good name."

"But is there proof?" Jack repeated. "Were there any witnesses, anyone who can back up Kami's version?"

"No one," Kami admitted with a sigh. "Rex took Alisa up the mountain to walk through her scene. That left just me, Hannah, and Lucy."

"Wait a minute — all we have to do is ask Hannah!" Alisa realized. She was ready to rush off and find her right there and then. "She's bound to remember Lucy checking Diabolo's cinch."

"Except that Hannah has been taken to the hospital in Boulder," Jack interrupted.

The girls stared at him, their faces filled with concern at this new information.

"She's doing fine," he reassured them, "but they wanted to check her out for a concussion. She'll be kept there overnight."

"Well, tomorrow then," Alisa insisted. Right now she realized she would have to refocus as she saw Rex approaching. "We'll be ready in five!" she told him, hurrying into the Stardust trailer to fetch Diabolo's tack.

"I'll help," Kami called after her.

The two girls got Diabolo ready while Rex and Jack talked quietly nearby.

"How's Mr. Peterson?" Jack asked. "Is he still mad at us?"

"I won't lie to you," Rex answered. "Your name is not exactly flavor of the month around here."

"But you talked him around," Jack remembered. "We have to thank you for that."

"No problem. I truly believe that Alisa and Diabolo can nail this next stunt in a way that no other horse and rider can. Besides, time is money when you're shooting a movie. The studio is putting pressure on Mr. Peterson to keep to schedule."

"You hear that?" Kami whispered to Alisa as she ran a brush through Diabolo's mane. "Rex believes in you!"

Alisa nodded, slipping the bit into Diabolo's mouth and easing the curb chain into place. "We'd better prove him right, huh?" she murmured.

Diabolo snorted and tossed her head, ready for action.

"Let's go," Rex told them, looking at his watch. "Mr. Peterson's up there ready to shoot the scene, and no way do you want to keep him waiting."

∽ ◦ ∾

Alisa rode Diabolo above the tree line. She looked back down the narrow trail they'd used, seeing the tiny trailers and tents below. Then she took in the rest of her surroundings — the jagged, snow-covered mountain peaks to the east and west, the glittering lakes nestled amidst forested slopes, and overhead a golden sun in a perfect blue sky.

Deep breath, she told herself. *Focus.*

There was the pointed finger of rock that she had to lope toward. One hundred and fifty feet down the slope, the technical crew was checking out camera positions and a gang of guys was unloading the last of fifty felled trees from the back of trailers and placing them in position. They hauled them upright with chains and pulleys, ready to set them alight when the director called for action — a fake forest fire, strictly controlled by a group of professional firefighters.

Snaking among the trees were fat, yellow hoses linked up to fire trucks. They would be ready to control the fire if the wind suddenly switched direction and drove the flames back down the mountain toward the natural tree line.

"Almost ready," Alisa whispered to Diabolo. She watched as the director gave last-minute instructions to his cameramen. He gave Rex a thumbs up.

The head wrangler strode toward them. "Time to take up your starting position," he told her, leading the way to a gap between two of the specially imported trees. "The guys will set the fire thirty feet to your left. You wait as long as you can, until the heat gets too much and you can see the helicopters. Then you and Diabolo take off up the mountain."

"Got it," Alisa nodded. She felt the tension in the air as every member of the team prepared for action. In the distance she heard the low rumble of approaching helicopters.

Diabolo, too, seemed to sense the atmosphere. She held her head high, her ears flicking in every direction. She swished her tail and pawed the ground.

"Easy," Alisa whispered as two of the guys in flame-retardant jackets stood ready to set the trees on fire.

Whoosh! And then *whoosh* again as they laid flaming torches against the base of the pine trees. Yellow flames began to lick up the straight, tall trunks. Alisa heard the crackle and spit of burning resin and saw fingers of bright flame leap up into the branches.

"Step back out of the shot, Rex," Jude's voice crackled out of Rex's walkie-talkie.

The wrangler raised a hand to pat Diabolo's neck, gave Alisa a reassuring smile, and retreated.

This was it; she took one last deep breath and waited for the director's cry.

"Action!"

The trees were ablaze; smoke spiraled into the clear blue sky. Diabolo flared her nostrils and waited, quivering as if on a knife-edge.

"Not yet," Alisa murmured. She had to wait until the heat grew too intense and the helicopters finally came over the ridge. The yellow flames turned to orange and then red. Sparks leaped in every direction. The blackened trunks began to twist and crack in the searing heat. Smoke filled her lungs and stung her eyes.

At last the helicopters came — one at a time, blades whirring, heavy bodies tilting as they lugged huge buckets of water suspended on long, swinging ropes — until finally there were five of them in shot.

"Go!" Alisa said, giving one small squeeze against Diabolo's sides.

Diabolo reared to paw the smoky air and then plunged forward through the fire and smoke, a shadowy shape captured by Peterson's cameras. The choppers began to release their watery cargo. The flames hissed and died, only to spring up again farther down the line.

"Faster!" Alisa urged.

Diabolo weaved in and out of the burning forest, ignoring the strange, churning beasts in the sky and the savage hiss of steam as the choppers spilled their water onto the inferno. She leaped over fallen branches with flames roaring in her ears and raced on up the mountain, almost blinded by the smoke that was everywhere. Alisa knew Diabolo would have to find her footing by instinct, trusting her rider to guide her to safety, so she crouched low. She ducked burning branches and steered Diabolo clear of a falling trunk. Meanwhile, firefighters began to swing down from the helicopters on ropes. Any second now Alisa and Diabolo would reach the clump of round rocks and the cool shadows of the deep ravine beyond. But first there was one more toppling tree to avoid, one more swirl of flames and shower of sparks . . .

"Cut!" Mike Peterson cried from way below.

And the firefighters moved in with their hoses to kill the flames.

∽ ◦ ᔢ

Alisa thought she would never get rid of the smell of smoke. It was in her nostrils, her clothes, her hair, and in Diabolo's saddle blanket and mane.

"I'll hose her down," Kami suggested, having stowed Magic safely inside the Stardust trailer. "You take a shower."

"I'll stay and help you," Alisa said. "My shower can wait."

Together the girls hosed Diabolo, gave her water, petted her, and made the biggest fuss.

"You were fantastic!" Kami threw both arms around the horse's neck while Alisa rubbed her dry. "I knew you and Alisa could do it," she whispered in her ear.

Diabolo accepted the praise calmly as if it was her due.

"Congratulations — good work." Jude smiled as he hurried by with a pile of scripts for tomorrow.

"Really terrific stunt," one of the cameramen added, unloading equipment from a nearby trailer. He saw Jack slinging Diabolo's saddle over a rail and hailed him to tell him not to worry about a thing. "Mr. Peterson's happy again," he assured him. "I even saw him smile."

Jack grinned back at the cameraman, but his expression quickly changed as he noticed Lucy and Pete Mason having a hard time trying to load Sapphire into the High Noon trailer. The pair was yanking at the horse's lead rope, trying to force the Appie up the ramp. Sapphire had firmly planted herself and was refusing to go in.

Kami and Alisa paused in their grooming of Diabolo as Jack walked over to the High Noon trailer.

"You need a hand?" he offered, his face showing no sign of the irritation he must have been feeling at Mason and Lucy's rough handling of their horse.

Pete Mason scowled back, but didn't bother to reply. Instead he handed the lead rope to Lucy, looped an extra rope behind Sapphire's butt, and began to pull on it like he was in an all-out tug of war. Lucy's horse raised her head and flattened her ears, rolling her eyes in fear.

"Maybe there's something inside the trailer she doesn't like?" Jack suggested.

"When I need advice from you, I'll ask," Mason grunted. He was sweating now from the effort of trying to force Sapphire into the trailer. "The horse is trailer-shy, period."

Lucy nodded in agreement. "I always have this problem. It goes way back. Sapphire and trailers, they don't mix."

The way they handle her, I'm not surprised, Kami thought. The poor Appaloosa's chest and belly were dark with sweat.

"So try easing off," Jack insisted, noticing chafe marks on Sapphire's haunches made by the thick rope.

That was the final straw for Mason. He flung down his rope and swore. Sapphire pulled hard on the lead rope, jerking it out of Lucy's hands and leaving her free to bolt from the trailer. She reared, turned, and ran to join Diabolo.

"Loser!" Lucy yelled at Jack. She stormed across the corral to fetch her horse. "And you!" she snapped at Alisa, who had calmly slipped a hand under Sapphire's halter. "You think you're such a big shot, Alisa Hamilton, but you're not. Anyone with half a brain can pull off the stunt you just shot!"

Alisa shook her head. Lucy was way out of line, but she was not about to listen to reason. There was no point in even trying.

"Me and Sapphire — we could've easily shot that scene. We're way better than you and your sorrel will ever be!"

"Don't kid yourself." Kami spoke up for Alisa. "Rex is right — Alisa and Diabolo are a special team. No one comes close."

Lucy snatched Sapphire away from Alisa. She almost spat out her parting words. "Yeah, well, you better make the most of your precious team while you can!"

"Wait!" Alisa frowned and followed her rival. "What do you mean, 'while we can'?"

Lucy stopped and gave a harsh laugh. "Don't pretend you don't know."

"Know what?" Alisa's heart skipped a beat.

"You're on Pete's list, Miss Nobody. At least, your horse is."

"Diabolo?" Alisa's heart lurched. She wanted to block her ears and not hear the rest of what Lucy was telling her.

"Diabolo is Pete's horse, and you'd better believe it."

Kami ran up and came between Lucy and Alisa. "Don't listen to her," she said as she tried to pull Alisa away.

Alisa ignored her. She glanced over to the High Noon trailer, where Jack was having angry words with Pete Mason. "You can't. I won't let you take her," she swore.

But Lucy refused to back down. There was a smile on her face as she delivered the final blow. "Believe me, this time next week you won't even be riding your precious horse."

"Nothing's been settled yet," Kami reminded Alisa.

"Yeah, Alisa, listen up." Lucy laughed. "Diabolo will be with us at High Noon. It'll be me on her back, not you!"

Chapter 10

Alisa was in shock. She felt numb, dazed, disorientated. She couldn't even get it together to lead Diabolo into the trailer — Kami had to do it for her.

All the way home from Estes Park she sat in stunned silence.

"Becca told us who was on the list, but we didn't want to tell you until you'd finished working on *Wildfire*," Kami told Alisa.

"Which was the right thing to do, considering the circumstances," agreed Jack. "It was important for you to keep your focus. Still, I wish Becca had kept quiet."

Alisa stared ahead at the flat, straight highway. Of course she'd known all along that Diabolo's future was at risk — how could she not? But somehow she'd blocked it out, told herself that Pete Mason would pick other horses at Stardust and leave Diabolo out of it. She'd even looked forward to working hard with the sorrel through the next summer and the one after that, putting in the extra effort to pull Stardust Stables back from the brink of disaster. "We will not be beaten!" she had murmured to Diabolo in the quiet dusk and in the sparkling dawn. "You and me — we'll get through this."

Now, as they pulled into the stable yard and Kami went to lower the trailer ramp, Alisa's heart was sore and her limbs felt heavy. Realizing that Jack's concerned gaze rested on her, she turned away.

"Hey," he said. "This isn't like you. You never give in without a fight."

Alisa replied with the faintest nod.

"Nothing's decided," Jack reminded her. "And we're going to make sure Mason doesn't win."

Another nod, then a shuddering intake of breath. How could they fight Pete Mason and his lawyer? Surely it was out of Stardust's hands.

"So take care of Diabolo," Jack said kindly but firmly.

It was exactly the right thing to say. Alisa climbed down from the cab and went around to the rear of the trailer, hardly noticing Kellie and Hayley still working in the round pen under floodlights with Dylan and Cool Kid. She stood aside to let Kami unload Magic, then she stepped up to fetch Diabolo.

"Hey, baby," she said quietly, untying her lead rope and leading her out. She heard the familiar clop of hooves against metal and felt her horse's warm breath as Diabolo nuzzled her shoulder.

Tell me what's wrong, Diabolo seemed to say.

Alisa shook her head, tethering Diabolo to the rail next to Magic and brushing her coat until she'd removed every speck of dust and Diabolo gleamed in the artificial glow cast by the lights in the pen. Then she brought food pellets from the barn and tipped them into a trough. "Eat," she told her horse.

Diabolo ignored the instruction and instead poked her nose into Alisa's face.

"Oh, baby," Alisa sighed, softly stroking the white blaze down Diabolo's face. "All I can say is, I love you."

Diabolo nuzzled Alisa's cheek.

∾ ◦ 𝒸𝓄

"Here comes the cavalry!" Becca drew back the curtain in the sitting area of the girls' dorm before breakfast next morning. "It's Dad!"

Kami, Kellie, and Hayley followed her out into the yard as a big white SUV pulled up and a gray-haired man in a suit stepped out. He was closely followed by a younger woman, also dressed for the office.

"And that must be Lizzie's attorney, Charlene Cross."

Still in bed, Alisa threw back her sheets and went to the window to look out. She saw the girls crowd around the visitors, then Lizzie and Jack emerging from the ranch house. Soon after, Zak and Tom came out of the barn, but she dressed slowly and hung back from joining the crowd, not daring to hope.

Out in the yard, Becca was making the formal introductions while Charlene Cross pulled documents out of her briefcase. "Lizzie, Jack — this is my dad, Simon Carter. There's nothing he doesn't know about divorce," Becca said proudly.

"It's good of you to come all this way," Lizzie said, shaking Simon's hand. "We know how busy you are."

"What else could I do?" he joked. "When my little princess calls me, I come running!"

"Yeah, Dad, whatever!" Becca laughed and blushed at the same time.

"Seriously, I hope there's something I can do

to help you all." Without even going inside the house, Simon immediately drew out a pair of reading glasses and started to leaf through the papers Charlene had given him. He talked as he read. "I know how much Becca loves working with Pepper here at Stardust. It means the world to her."

"Me, too," Kellie chipped in. "Even though Dylan's not on Mason's list, I definitely don't want him to get his hands on any of our horses."

"Me, neither," came a quiet chorus of voices.

"We're all agreed — we have to stop this from happening," Charlene said briskly. She then suggested to Lizzie and Jack that they go indoors to talk. The young stunt riders were left hanging out on the front porch.

"Where's Alisa?" Becca noticed that their group was incomplete, so she went to haul Alisa out of the dorms. "You need to come and join us," she told her. Alisa was slowly pulling on her leather boots.

"I'm on my way."

Becca swept her blond hair back from her face and looked quizzically at Alisa. "I thought you'd be the first one out there."

"I said I'm coming." The night hadn't made things better for Alisa. She had tossed and turned all night, barely sleeping a wink. If anything, this morning she felt more heart-sore and weary. Her whole body seemed drained of energy.

"If anyone can do this, my dad can," Becca insisted. She sat by Alisa on the edge of her bed. There was a pause before she went on. "I know that we're not best buddies and that's because you and I often go head to head whenever a big job comes up. But I care about Stardust and all the horses here just as much as you do."

"I know."

"I really do. I love Pepper more than anything, just like you love Diabolo."

Tears began to prick Alisa's eyes as she finally looked up at Becca.

"I'd do anything not to lose Pepper. How about you?"

"Likewise," Alisa agreed, brushing away her tears. "Thanks, Becca."

"For what?"

Alisa stood up, smiled briefly, then reached for her hat. "Just, thanks."

∽ ◦ ᥑ

"So, no trip up to Estes Park today?" Tom asked Kami.

It was noon, and the sun was shining bright in the crystal blue sky. The two riders were in the red-roofed barn tossing hay bales down from the top of the stack onto the flat bed of the tractor-trailer.

"Diabolo and Alisa have the day off," she told him. "We go again tomorrow."

Tom hauled a bale off the top and let it drop to the ground. "So, tell me about the scene where they set fire to the forest."

"It was pretty cool," Kami said with a grin. "They set it up so well — it looked completely real. And Diabolo was amazing." Since the arrival of Becca's dad early that morning, Kami and the rest of the Stardust team had thrown themselves into work, scooping poop, cleaning tack, and shifting the bales.

"All the horses here are amazing," Tom went on. "Every single one. That's why we have to fight Mason."

None of the young riders knew exactly what Simon Carter had discussed with Lizzie and Jack, or whether there was any reason to hope. Still, it didn't stop Tom from sounding completely determined.

Pushing another heavy bale to the edge of the stack, Kami gave it a swift kick and watched it topple down. A cloud of dust rose as the bale landed with a heavy thud. "Are you thanking your lucky stars that Legend isn't on the list?" she asked.

"I sure am," Tom replied quietly.

"I wish I was in your shoes."

"I know," he told her. "Do you want to talk about it?"

"Later, maybe." Right now all Kami wanted to do was to stay busy.

"Whenever you're ready," Tom told her. And together they hauled another bale.

∽ ◦ ⌒

The next day, Jack asked Kami to load Magic in the trailer and drive up with Alisa and him to Estes Park, as usual.

"Alisa needs backup," he explained. "And she really appreciates you being there."

"I know she does," Kami agreed. "Plus, we have to get proof that Lucy was the one who loosened Hannah's cinch."

Jack shrugged. "That won't be easy," he warned her. "Besides, today is going to be a hard day for Alisa. She has to work alongside Lucy on a stunt — Alisa and Diabolo, Lucy and Sapphire performing Roman riding and saddle falls. It's going to be pretty tense."

They got the trailer ready, then ate a big, hearty breakfast. By the time the sun was up over Clearwater Peak, Diabolo and Magic were loaded in the trailer and the *Wildfire* team was ready to hit the road.

"Call me if there's any news from Becca's dad," Jack told Lizzie as she came out to wave them off.

"It'll take more than twenty-four hours for him and Charlene to go through the paperwork," Lizzie warned. "They have to look at all our bank statements and the contracts we signed relating to the ownership of Stardust. There's a heap of stuff to go through. And there's a problem — I can't seem to find some of the most important documents."

"Do you think you lost them?" Jack wondered.

Lizzie frowned. "Or else Pete took them with him when he moved out. That's possible, I guess."

"Let's just try and focus on the day ahead," Jack told Alisa and Kami as they left Stardust Stables. The road north was long and straight, keeping west of Denver and heading on toward Boulder. "We act like nothing's happened," he added after a few moments of silence. His hands were steady on the steering wheel and his voice was firm.

"That's the hard part," Kami protested, remembering the vicious look on Lucy's face and the cruelty of Pete Mason's handling of Sapphire.

"But we're professionals," he insisted. "We have to stay calm and do our job."

∿ ◦ ∾

As always, Jack's advice was good.

They arrived on location with only thirty minutes before Rex was going to walk the stunt riders through the day's shoot. That meant a quick unloading of the horses and tack, followed by a thorough grooming, then five minutes to lead Magic and Diabolo to water in the big trough in the corner of the corral.

"I can't see the High Noon trailer," Alisa commented with ten minutes to go. "They should be here by now."

"Maybe they broke down," Kami suggested. Part of her was glad at the idea of not having to face Lucy and Mason, but she also felt a flicker of fear. "I hope they didn't have an accident."

But just then the flashy silver trailer came speeding up the dirt road, bumping over rocks and dipping into deep ruts made by the heavy vehicles belonging to the technical crews.

"Ouch!" Alisa grimaced as Pete Mason put on the brakes and squealed to a halt.

A few minutes later, he and Lucy had unloaded Sapphire and tied her to the rail.

"Just look at that poor horse!" Kami muttered under her breath.

Lucy's Appie was sweating from the journey and resisting Lucy's attempts to put a bit in her mouth. She had only just succeeded when Rex showed up.

Mason had been speaking agitatedly into his phone, but he quickly broke off and offered to go with Lucy and Alisa while Rex talked them through the morning's stunts. This left Jack and Kami to take care of the horses, and Jack grabbed the chance to loosen Sapphire's tether.

Kami was settling Diabolo and Magic when Jude Amery hurried up.

"Hannah just sent me a text," he told Kami.

"Is she out of the hospital?"

"Yeah, they gave her the all-clear yesterday, which is good news — she shoots two important scenes later today, and we can't wait if we want to stay on schedule," Jude explained. "Anyway she asked me to pass on a message to you and Alisa."

"Alisa's busy right now. What does Hannah want?" Kami kept her fingers crossed. *Please don't let Hannah be mad at us over her accident!*

"For you to meet her in her trailer. It's urgent."

"Does she say what it's about?" Kami asked, a little worried.

"No."

"So, should I wait for Alisa?"

"No. I would just go straight there." Jude himself was very busy preparing for the day's shoot and wanted to move on to the next task. "It's the third trailer on the left, under those pine trees. Don't worry, Hannah won't bite."

Chapter 11

"So, today's stunt has nothing to do with fire," Rex explained. He stood with Pete Mason, Lucy, and Alisa in the clearing with the shack where Alisa had first worked on jumping the razor-wire fence.

"This is the scene where Lucy does her favorite trick, right?" Pete Mason spoke up for his rider, who looked cool and confident.

"Roman riding," Rex confirmed. "This is how it goes. Alisa, your character is leading Lucy's character into the clearing when your horse spooks for no reason. She throws you clean out of the saddle, but your right foot catches in the stirrup and you're dragged along."

"A one-foot drag," Pete Mason confirmed in a tone that said this stunt was everyday, beginner's stuff.

Rex paced out the action. "Then, Lucy, this is

where your character comes in. Sapphire lopes up alongside Alisa and Diabolo. You raise yourself out of the saddle and squat on his haunches, letting go of the reins. Then, after three strides, you step astride Diabolo and ease into her saddle. You rein Diabolo back, at the same time hauling Alisa out of the dirt. You both end up on Alisa's horse, right?"

"Cool," Lucy confirmed.

Yeah, cool, but this'll take perfect teamwork, Alisa thought with a slight shudder. With anyone except Lucy Reeves, she would have been totally happy.

❧ ◦ ☙

"Come right in." Hannah stuck her head out of the trailer window as Kami stepped nervously up to the door with the star's name on it.

Friendly enough so far, Kami thought. It didn't feel as if Hannah was about to vent over her so-called accident.

"Don't look so freaked out," Hannah smiled. "What happened the other day wasn't your fault. Now sit; have a soda."

Kami took the drink and sank into a soft couch with a cowboy motif printed on cream-colored, velvety fabric. The whole interior followed a Western theme, with silver spurs, Stetsons, sheriff's stars, and lassos hanging from the walls.

"Look — I didn't get hurt!" Hannah twirled in the confined space to show that she was one hundred percent okay. "I just knocked my stupid head — doh! But the doctors said there'll be no long-term effects. The only downside is the legal guys at Diamond Studios have ordered no more horse riding for me, or else. So I guess that's the end of my short and inglorious cowgirl career."

"We were worried," Kami confessed.

"No need. And I don't want you and Alisa to feel bad."

"We do, though."

Hannah sat down next to Kami. "That's what I figured. I heard that Mr. Peterson gave your outfit a hard time. So I decided to put him right."

Kami's eyes opened wide. She couldn't imagine anyone daring to challenge the all-powerful movie director.

"As soon as I got back, I went to his trailer and told him — 'The last person to check my cinch before my accident was Lucy Reeves.'"

"Jeez! And what did he say?"

"You know these movie big shots — they

move on from one multi-million dollar issue to another in the blink of an eye. Once he learned from the medics that I didn't seriously injure myself, he just let the entire thing drop."

"But at least you told him the truth." A flood of relief washed over Kami. "Thanks, Hannah. Seriously, thank you. You were our only witness; we were relying on you."

"No problem." The star smiled sweetly. "Then I told Rex the same thing, and he made sure the news spread through the whole crew. We're not saying that Lucy did it deliberately, by the way."

Kami nodded. "That'd be hard to prove."

"So, let's say it might not have been sabotage. Maybe it was just pure carelessness. Anyway, you and Alisa are definitely off the hook."

"I don't know what it is with Lucy," Kami confessed. "Alisa never did anything to upset her, but from the moment Lucy came out to Estes Park, she's been gunning for her."

"To me, it's obvious," Hannah argued. "Alisa is the better rider — period."

"And Lucy can't stomach it?"

"Exactly. That's all it takes for someone with hidden insecurities like Lucy to start making trouble. I'm not blind, I've seen how she's been acting."

"Lucy Reeves, insecure?" Kami asked with disbelief.

Hannah nodded. "She has to be the best. When she's not, she goes into meltdown, hence her attitude problem toward Alisa. So anyway, I wasn't through yet. After I let everyone know about her messing with my cinch, I went online and found the U.S. stunt register. That's the place where everyone who holds a license to stunt-ride is listed. And guess what — Lucy's name isn't there."

"No license," Kami repeated. She herself was still racking up the sixty hours in front of the camera needed to gain a license. Then there was a tough riding test with a member of the Screen Actors' Guild before you got the right to appear on the register. Meanwhile, you picked up as much work experience as you could at a lower rate of pay.

"But look at this." Unfolding a sheet of paper, Hannah showed Kami a copy of Lucy's résumé.

The paper showed a cute close-up of a smiling Lucy wearing a straw Stetson and multiple strings of turquoise beads. Above the picture were words in bold print: "Lucy Reeves, Junior Stunt Rider for World-famous High Noon Stables." Then in smaller letters — "Age 15. Winner of interstate barrel-racing and reining contests, member of the U.S. Olympic training squad, registered with the Screen Actors' Guild."

"Interesting, hey?"

"Yeah, the Guild runs the stunt register," Kami agreed. "Can I keep this?"

"Sure," Hannah told her. "And I'm officially inviting you and Alisa to the wrap party in Denver after we're through filming. It'd be great to see you both there."

∽ ◦ ⌒

Back on set, Pete Mason was bending Mike Peterson's ear.

"Roman riding is a tough stunt to pull off," he insisted. "Lucy's been working on it a lot, though. At High Noon we have four junior riders at her level. That's more than any other stunt-riding stable."

"Get ready to shoot in three," Mike Peterson told Jude, who ran to inform Rex and the two girls. Alisa and Lucy were waiting with their horses at the edge of the clearing.

"We're a top-notch stable," Pete Mason continued. "Right now we're increasing the number of highly trained horses on our string —

soon there'll be nobody in the whole of Colorado bigger or better than us."

"Speak with Rex." Mr. Peterson was curt with the owner of High Noon, almost physically pushing him to one side. "He's head wrangler."

"Two minutes," Jude told the girls. "Lucy, you hold Sapphire back until Alisa and Diabolo reach the rock that's shaped like a turtle. You watch her take the fall and go into her one-foot drag. That's when you launch into action. Everyone set?"

Nerves tingling, Alisa nodded and took deep breaths to calm herself. Then she went through every stage of the stunt in her mind: the exact number of strides Diabolo would take to get to the rock before she threw herself sideways and hung from the saddle with her body just skimming the ground. Five seconds holding the drag before Lucy loped up on Sapphire and stood astride the two horses. Three more strides before Lucy hauled her upright again.

Glancing sideways and catching Lucy in profile, she saw beads of sweat on her fellow rider's forehead.

"One minute!" Jude said before he and Rex retreated out of shot.

"You okay?" Alisa asked Lucy.

Picking up on her rider's nervousness,

Sapphire took a couple of skittish steps to the side, almost knocking into Alisa and Diabolo.

"I'm fine," Lucy muttered fiercely.

"Easy, baby," Alisa told Diabolo. "Everything's going to be fine."

The countdown from ten began. *Eight, seven, six . . .*

"You reach up with your free hand to catch my arm, and then I haul you up — okay!" Lucy had left it late to run through the details.

Alisa nodded, but there was a knot in her stomach and more than the usual butterflies.

Three, two, one . . .

"Action!"

At the slightest shift of weight from her rider, Diabolo broke into a smooth, easy lope, unworried by the team of cameramen and sound technicians stationed in the clearing. She looked beautiful in the dappled sunlight and she clearly knew it. When she reached the turtle rock and Alisa launched herself from the saddle, she didn't even break stride.

Alisa threw herself sideways and the whizzing world turned upside down. Rocks and grass were where the sky should be, and trees and clouds were under her feet. *Go, Lucy!* she thought as Diabolo sped on.

She heard hooves coming up from behind, felt rather than saw Lucy free herself from her stirrups and slide out of the saddle. By now she must be crouching on Sapphire's haunches, ready to switch her balance and stand astride the two horses. Alisa saw everything in a distorted blur.

Yes! Lucy had got through the hardest part of the stunt. Now she was easing forward into Diabolo's saddle, and Alisa was ready to stretch up with her free hand. She groped upward for Lucy's outstretched arm. There was nothing there. "Give me your hand!" she whispered.

Then she heard a yell. Lucy had leaned out too far and lost her balance. There was a thud, and Lucy hit the ground, almost dislodging Alisa's foot from the stirrup as she fell.

"Cut!" Peterson yelled angrily.

Riderless, Sapphire loped to the far side of the clearing while Diabolo, realizing that the trick had misfired, right away put on the brakes. Now all Alisa could do was grasp hold of the saddle horn, pull herself back up, then reach forward and grab the flying reins. "Whoa!" she told Diabolo.

Her brilliant horse stopped almost immediately, even though Sapphire charged on ahead.

"Hold it!" Alisa whispered. She gently turned Diabolo around to check on the scene behind them.

She saw Lucy curled up on her side, clutching her elbow. Jude, Rex, and Pete Mason were running across the clearing to help.

"Okay," she told Diabolo. "Lucy's got some help. What we have to do is go after that runaway horse!"

∽ ◦ ⌒

By the time Alisa and Diabolo set off in pursuit, the rangy Appie was already well out of sight.

"This way," she muttered, picking up Sapphire's prints in the sandy ground. She bent low to avoid thick branches, jumped fallen trunks, and skirted around rocky outcrops, hot on the trail.

"That poor horse must be crazy with fear," Alisa said out loud. "Out here on the mountain, all alone."

Diabolo nickered then swung left around a stunted tree. The brim of Alisa's hat caught on a branch, and she had to jam it back on her head to stop it from falling in the dirt. When she looked up again, she saw that they'd come to a wide slab of solid granite.

"Whoa, easy. This is where the track ends," she said. There were no hoof prints to follow, no sign of which direction Sapphire might have gone.

Diabolo stopped dead at the edge of the rocky platform. Then she threw back her head and gave an ear-splitting whinny. Once, twice, three times.

"What can you hear?" Alisa whispered in the silence that followed.

At first there was nothing but the wind in the trees.

"Again?" she asked.

But there was no need. Diabolo waited until at last another horse farther up the mountain whinnied back — the faint call of a fellow creature who was lost and scared.

"We hear you!" Alisa called. She let Diabolo pick her way through a patch of aspens to the left of the granite platform.

Up they loped, through more aspens in their shimmering, summer glory, across a clearing toward a final cluster of pines. Diabolo carried Alisa into the shade of the tall trees and then stopped.

It took a while for Alisa's eyes to get used

to the dim light; she sensed Sapphire's presence before she actually saw her. There she was, backed against a tall rock, sweated up, and breathing heavily. She was watching their approach, ready to flee again.

"Easy, girl," Alisa murmured. She saw that Lucy's horse was exhausted and unlikely to run if they went up quietly, without scaring her. "We're here to help."

Sapphire rolled her eyes and laid back her ears in warning. Diabolo lowered her head and blew gently through her lips.

They were close now, near enough to see the flecks of foam at the corners of Sapphire's mouth and within reach of her trailing reins.

Alisa eased her weight sideways in the saddle and stretched out her hand. "We're not going to hurt you," she promised.

Sapphire shook as Alisa took hold of the reins, but she didn't spook. She held still and let Diabolo and Alisa into her space.

"Good girl, let's take you home," Alisa murmured with a long sigh of relief.

Chapter 12

"That's it — you two are through." Rex was stern and unbending as he fired the High Noon duo from the *Wildfire* shoot.

With a red face, Mason was ready to protest, but Rex cut him off. "You want a list of reasons? First off, Lucy lied about her qualifications. Worse, she messed with Hannah's cinch."

"I didn't mean —" Lucy began.

"I'm not even listening!" Rex warned her. "Only you and your conscience know if you loosened that cinch deliberately, but that's not the issue. Here's the deal — you're fired!"

A dozen people stood listening in the yard where the trailers were parked, with the sun past its midday height and shadows beginning to lengthen.

"You can't fire us. We have a contract." Mason finally got in a sentence. He was angry, and he knew that they were in the wrong, but he wasn't ready to lose the job.

Rex's steely stare drilled into him. "The contract is based on your rider being trained to perform all the stunts we ask her to do, and she definitely is not."

"Jeez, this is really awful," Kami whispered to Alisa and Jack as they stood on the sidelines along with Jude and other members of the crew. None of the Stardust team took any pleasure in seeing Lucy humiliated.

They tried not to stare too hard. Lucy was holding Sapphire's lead rope with the arm that wasn't strapped up from wrist to elbow. She had turned bright red with shame.

"I'd feel a whole lot more sorry for her if she didn't treat her horse so badly," Jack reminded them.

It had taken Alisa and Diabolo two whole hours to guide Sapphire back down the mountain to the clearing where Rex had greeted them. He'd taken over and walked Sapphire to the corral.

Now there was no room for Mason to bluster and wriggle his way out — High Noon Stables was no longer part of the *Wildfire* movie.

"Okay, we're out of here." Lucy was the first to back down, still unable to meet Alisa and

Kami's gaze as she struggled to load Sapphire into the trailer.

Jack stepped in, taking the rope and leading the Appie in without fuss. Then he checked that there was a full hay net and enough water for the journey home.

Meanwhile, Rex made sure that Mason fully understood his position. "I won't be passing your name on to people in the business any time soon," he warned. "I know a lot of guys who hire stunt riders, and your outfit won't be high on their list."

Scowling, Mason clenched and unclenched his fists. "Who needs you?" he muttered, casting a glance of pure loathing at Jack as he came out of the High Noon trailer. "We're big, and we're about to get bigger."

Kami and Alisa swallowed hard. Lucy and Mason might be off the movie, but that didn't mean Stardust's other problem would just vanish. They watched as Mason turned on his heel and yelled at Lucy to get in the cab. He muttered under his breath as he raised the trailer ramp and bolted it shut. In less than a minute, he'd reversed out of his parking spot, crossed the lot with squealing tires, and jolted onto the dirt road.

The last they saw of the High Noon team was

the back of the silver vehicle disappearing in a cloud of dust.

"Which leaves us with a problem," Rex commented. He thought for a while, then turned and spoke to a woman who worked in the costume department. "Eva, have you got a dark wig we could use?"

Eva nodded and right away went to fetch it, leaving Kami and Alisa wondering what was coming next.

Rex strolled across to Kami. "You brought your horse along with you?"

"Yeah."

"Would you mind being brunette for a day?"

"No." *Is Rex asking what I think he's asking? No, he couldn't be.*

"Jack, what's your opinion? Can your two riders perform the Roman riding trick up in the clearing?"

"Better ask Kami." Jack smiled at her and winked.

"Kami, can you and your horse stand in for Lucy and Sapphire?"

Kami's face lit up. "Sure! Just show us where to start."

∽ ◦ ℃

"Ready?" Alisa beamed at Kami as they both sat at the edge of the green clearing in the forest.

"Totally." Kami grinned back. It was her dream come true — to be riding Magic alongside Alisa and Diabolo on a major movie. "Just pinch me to tell me I'm not dreaming," she added.

"We can nail this," Alisa assured her. She loved Kami's raw enthusiasm, her joy in doing the job.

Rex gave the cinches one last check before stepping back.

"Three, two, one . . ." Jude counted.

"Action!"

At Mr. Peterson's command, Alisa set Diabolo into a fast lope. Sure, there were butterflies in her stomach, but not like before with Lucy. This time it was pure adrenaline coursing through her veins.

The second she reached the turtle rock and heard Kami burst into action, Alisa launched herself out of the saddle and went into her spectacular one-foot drag while Diabolo kept a steady course across the clearing. Kami and Magic gained on them. Then Kami, too, was out of the saddle, crouched on Magic's haunches, stepping astride the two horses, who loped in perfect unison. Then she was across the gap, safe in Diabolo's saddle, and reaching out for Alisa's hand. Quick as a flash, Kami swung Alisa up behind her and she felt Alisa's arms clasped around her waist.

"Cut!" the director called.

∽ ◦ ᄋ

"You should've seen Magic fly across the clearing!" That night by Elk Creek, an exhausted but ecstatic Kami gave Kellie, Becca, and Hayley a blow-by-blow account. "He didn't make one mistake."

"Likewise with Diabolo," Alisa added. It had been a long drive back from Estes Park. She was so tired she could hardly stay awake to eat, even though Zak, Tom, and some of the other guys had organized a cookout specially for her and Kami. "We even got another smile from Mr. Peterson."

"He shook our hands," Kami said. "Can you believe it — he told us 'good job'!"

"What did Jack say?" Hayley wanted to know.

"He said we were half a second off on our timing," Alisa chuckled. "I guess we still have work to do."

"Typical Jack," Tom said with a smile, reaching for the barbecue sauce.

"So, Becca, any news from your dad?" It was Kami who voiced the question that was on everyone's mind.

"Nothing yet." Pulling out her phone, Becca checked her texts. "Nope. No message."

For a while, everyone was busy heaping food on their plates and going down to the creek to eat. Kami met up with Hayley to tell her more about the day while Alisa joined Tom and Zak.

"How cute is that?" She pointed across the stream to the horses in the meadow. "See, at the feeder? Diabolo is shoving Legend and Liberty out of the way to make room for Magic. They're definitely best friends."

Everyone was going back for second helpings when Zak heard a vehicle approaching in the distance. "Visitors at this time of night?" he commented. The moon was already rising, and stars were beginning to twinkle in the vast sky.

Tom was the first to recognize Pete Mason's trailer when it rounded the bend. "What the heck!" he muttered.

Soon everyone had left the peaceful creek and gathered anxiously in the yard. Jack and Lizzie appeared on the ranch-house porch.

Mason's headlights raked across the meadow. He drove too fast for the dirt road, spitting up small rocks and rattling over washouts. When he finally pulled up in the yard, Jack and Lizzie strode to meet him.

"Pete, it's kind of late," Jack began.

"Don't worry, this is not a social visit," Mason muttered, clutching a letter as he slid from the cab and swayed unsteadily. Ignoring Lizzie's husband, Mason thrust the letter into his ex-wife's hand. "I've come for my horses — it's all legal."

The slurred words stunned the young stunt riders. It was what they'd all been dreading.

"Magic!" Kami's first instinct was to turn and fetch him out of the meadow and take him as far away from there as possible, but Tom held her back.

Meanwhile, Alisa turned to Becca. "He can't do this, can he?" she said in alarm.

"We don't know what it says in the letter," Becca said faintly.

"From my attorney," Mason told Lizzie. "It's all the proof I need to trailer those six horses back to High Noon."

Kami struggled free from Tom and then set off at a run toward the bridge that crossed the creek. "I won't let him," she vowed, glancing over her shoulder to see that Hayley and Kellie were following behind her.

Back in the yard, Mason muttered something to Jack that made him so angry that he lashed out with his fist. The punch missed Mason's jaw by an inch.

"Call your dad," Alisa told Becca, her heart racing. "Tell him what's happening."

"Stay out of my way," Mason warned Lizzie as she stepped in between him and Jack.

"You call this proof!" she cried, holding up the crumpled piece of paper. "This is nothing. This is just the lying statement you made to your original two-bit attorney."

"It's enough," Mason bullied, thrusting her to one side. Then he lurched off toward the footbridge with Tom and Zak close on his heels. "I'm here for my horses and no one's going to stop me."

"Becca — your dad!" Alisa insisted, urging her to make the call.

"It's no good, his phone's turned off," Becca reported a moment later. "Or else there's no signal."

"So, we join the others," Alisa decided. "He's one man against all of us. We can stop him."

"The guy's crazy," Becca warned.

Crazy or not, Mason was definitely a man on a mission. He crossed the rickety bridge into the meadow and headed straight for the gate. While Kami, Kellie, and Hayley herded as many of their horses as they could into the farthest corner, Tom and Zak caught up with Mason and stood between him and the gate. But they were no match for Pete Mason. He swiped them aside and grabbed the metal handle. Seconds later, the gate swung wide open.

"It's total chaos!" Becca panicked. Lizzie and Jack had stayed behind to call Charlene Cross and the cops. She and Alisa were the last on the scene. "These horses are so spooked they'll probably make a run for it."

Sure enough, Kami, Kellie, and Hayley couldn't contain the horses. It was Jack's Liberty who broke away first, then Lizzie's Sugar, quickly followed by Cool Kid and Ziggy. Pretty soon they had a full-blown stampede on their hands.

"Magic, no — come back!" Kami picked out her horse's pale gray shape running with the rest of the herd. Hooves thundered and manes flew as the horses galloped back and forth in the confined space.

"Come back!" Kami repeated.

Magic broke his stride and split from the herd to join Kami.

Over by the gate, Mason held Tom and Zak at

bay. He lunged and laughed cruelly, ignoring the warning yells of Alisa and Becca.

"Get out of the way!" Becca cried when she saw that Mason was standing right in the path of the stampeding herd. "If he stays where he is, sooner or later they'll run right through him!"

Alisa called for Diabolo, who loped uncertainly after the lead horses. "Here, baby, it's me. Come to me."

Through the thundering hooves and angry yells, Diabolo pricked up her ears. The white flash running the length of her face stood out in the moonlight as she turned her head.

"Come on, baby," Alisa urged.

As Diabolo joined Alisa; Tom, Zak, Kellie, and Hayley hurried to regroup. Standing with their arms linked to form a human barrier, they managed to steer the stampede away from the open gate. As the horses veered off to the left, they passed so close to Mason that Liberty's back foot caught him a glancing blow. He swore and staggered sideways.

"Good girl, Diabolo." Alisa's soft, persistent words kept her sorrel close by her side.

"Easy, Magic," Kami murmured. She stroked his neck and eased herself up on to his back.

Alisa vaulted smoothly on to Diabolo and

held him steady alongside Kami and Magic. "That's it. Now we four are going to stop all this craziness. We're going to do what the guys on foot aren't able to do because Mason is standing in their way — we're going to close the gate."

With every sinew straining, ears laid flat against their heads, Diabolo and Magic waited the short time it took for Alisa and Kami to turn them toward the gate. Without saddle or bridle, the girls grasped chunks of mane and then clicked their tongues.

"We don't have much time," Kami murmured.

Across the meadow, Liberty was swinging the herd around again. This was a classic fight or flight situation. The horses felt trapped and under threat and so had only one joint idea — freedom!

"We've got to move fast!" Alisa urged, and she and Kami galloped Diabolo and Magic under the moon in a race to the gate. The stampeding horses were barreling back toward the gate, running flat out. Becca had grabbed Mason by the arm and was trying to haul him out of the way, but Mason was still resisting.

Alisa and Kami crouched low and clung to their horses' manes. They were almost there, aiming at the narrow gap between Mason's back and the open gate. Yes — they leaned sideways and grasped the cold metal. Summoning all their strength, they swung the gate on its hinges!

It crashed shut with only a few feet to spare before the horses reached it. Dusty, sweating, and breathing hard, the herd pulled up at the barrier. Crisis averted — the Stardust team had done it!

Chapter 13

"Now this," said Becca, holding up her iPad to show the email she'd just received, "is what you call proof!"

It was Saturday night — the end of a long, eventful week. The *Wildfire* shoot was over, and the crisis caused by Pete Mason's unwelcome visit had come and gone. The cops had arrived and hauled him off in their car. Now all the Stardust gang was gathered in the big ranch-house dining room waiting for Jack's mouth-watering, world-famous supper: leg of beef slow-roasted in the oven and served with mountains of French fries, other vegetables optional.

Alisa and Kami sat quietly in the window seat. They held back while the others crowded around Becca's iPad.

"It's from my dad," Becca announced. "He says he's just emailed Jack and Lizzie to let them know that the horses are safe." She scanned the email. "He and Charlene found documents signed by Mason way before the divorce. Lizzie was right about her ex sneaking them out when they split up. And naturally he didn't hand them over to Bradley Stewart because they proved he'd given up his claim to the horses at Stardust. But Dad put pressure on Mason's attorney to quiz his client about the papers he'd stolen, and in the end Mason caved in and admitted it — the rat!"

"The missing documents prove that Mason gave up any claims he might have had on Stardust while he and Lizzie were still married. At the time Lizzie got him to sign them, Mason's real estate business was going broke, so the only way she could save Stardust was to take sole ownership."

Becca, Zak, and Tom rushed over to Kami and Alisa, all speaking at once.

"Did you hear that?"

"Mason lied like he always does."

"He has no claim. He's not taking our horses anywhere. They're staying right where they are." Becca stared, wide-eyed, at Kami and Alisa.

So good! Alisa closed her eyes and took time to let the news sink in, while Kami jumped up and hugged everyone within reach.

"Magic can stay!" she cried, hugging Tom.

Tom hugged Kami right back and then planted a soft kiss on her forehead.

Kellie saw the kiss, grinned, then moved on. "So, we can all carry on working together — this year, next year . . . for as long as Jack and Lizzie will have us."

Opening her eyes, Alisa smiled and nodded. "That's because of you, Becca," she said. "So, thank you, from the bottom of all our hearts."

"Hey, no problem!" Becca said, heading for the door. "I'd better go and make sure that Jack and Lizzie have checked their email!"

"Phew, huh?" Kami walked over to Alisa. Her short question just about said it all.

"Yeah, phew." Alisa smiled and stood up. "Tell Jack I'm going to skip the roast tonight."

"You must be exhausted." Kami sighed. "After the week you've had, I'm not surprised."

Alisa nodded. Every muscle in her body ached and her brain cells had pretty much given up on her. It was time to lay her head on her pillow. "And I'm on the early shift tomorrow, bringing in the horses. So I'm ready to tell everyone goodnight."

"Goodnight," Kami told her quietly, watching her as she went.

"Walk?" Tom suggested.

Kami nodded. The crescent moon was low over the horizon as they strolled by the creek.

On the way out of the dining room, Alisa had given high-fives to Kellie and Hayley. "All the horses get to stay here at Stardust!" Kellie had said over and over, gray eyes sparkling with joy.

Out in the hallway, Alisa took her hat from the stand and zipped up her jacket. She was tired, but not too tired to walk out to the meadow and talk to her horse — never too tired for that. So she crossed the yard and then the corral. As she crossed the footbridge, she paused to gaze down at the clear, gurgling water. She looked up to see Diabolo steadily weaving through the herd to meet her.

"Hey, baby," she called, then delivered her own verdict on their performance on the *Wildfire* set. "Pretty much an A-list star, huh?"

Diabolo came close and nuzzled Alisa's arm. Here they were in the moonlight, with not a care in the world, totally at ease.

"We were awesome." Alisa grinned, recalling the one-foot drag, the Roman riding with Kami and Magic, and the solo running through smoke and flames. As she rested her head against Diabolo's neck, she imagined their next adventure.

She stayed there a long time under the moon and stars. Tomorrow there would be work to do: scooping, brushing, feeding, and more training in the round pen. But tonight all she needed to do was loop her arm around Diabolo's neck, tell her how much she loved her, and then sleep.

About the Author

Sable Hamilton is the pen name for Jenny Oldfield, author of a wide range of books for children and young adults — including the internationally successful mini series Beautiful Dead and Dark Angel. With Stardust Stables, she has returned to one of her favorite subjects — the glamour, the thrills, and the trials of working with horses!

Glossary

admiration (ad-mir-AY-shun) — the feeling of really liking and respecting someone

concentrate (KAHN-suhn-trate) — to focus your thoughts and attention on one thing

concussion (kuhn-KUHSH-uhn) — an injury to the head from a heavy hit

demonstrate (DEM-uhn-strate) — to show how to do something, to show something clearly

exhausted (ig-ZAWST-ed) — feeling very tired

immaculately (i-MAK-yuh-lit-lee) — doing something carefully and neatly

partition (pahr-TISH-uhn) — a panel that divides a room or area

resist (ri-ZIST) — to fight back and struggle because you do not want to do something

sabotage (SAB-uh-tahzh) — damaging property or doing something bad on purpose in order to stop something from happening

scrutinize (SKROO-tuh-nize) — to look over closely and carefully

skittish (SKIT-ish) — very nervous, easily frightened, and hard to control

More about Horses

bridle (BRYE-duhl) — a harness that goes on a horse's head, which allows a person to control and guide it

currycomb (KUR-ee-kom) — a type of comb with plastic ridges used to get dirt and other things out of a horse's coat

halter (HAWL-tur) — a strap that fits behind the ears and over the nose, used to lead or tie up an animal like a horse

lope (LOHP) — a Western term for canter, but may be more easy-going and relaxed than a canter

sorrel (SOR-uhl) — a horse that is reddish brown with a mane and tail of the same or lighter color

tack (TAK) — all of the things you need to ride a horse, like a saddle and bridle

trot (TRAHT) — a speed that's in between walking and running, slower than a canter or gallop

warmblood (WAWRM-bluhd) — a type of horse that includes many different breeds, known for being easy to ride and having good speed and endurance

Discussion Questions

1. Do you think Lucy purposefully loosened the cinch on Diabolo's saddle, or was it an accident? Try to use examples from the book to support your answer.

2. Becca found out which horses Pete Mason wanted to take, but the other riders made her promise not to tell Alisa that Diablo was on the list. Was is it okay for them to not tell Alisa? Why or why not?

3. Talk about some possible reasons that Sapphire, Lucy's horse, was so skittish.

Writing Prompts

1. Making a movie takes a lot of teamwork, and the Stardust Stable riders also have to work together. Write about a time when you had to work in a team to get something done.

2. Write a story about what would have happened if Pete Mason had gotten the rights to take half of the horses from Stardust Stables.

3. Which would you rather be, a stunt rider or an actor? Write about and explain your choice.

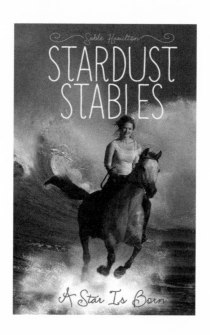

A Star Is Born

Kami is super excited about joining Stardust Stables and quickly falls in love with her gorgeous horse, Magic. When the chance arises to try out for the role of stunt double to starlet Coreen Kessler, her dreams are close to coming true! Kami knows she has a good shot at getting the part — but so does seasoned stunt rider Becca, and there's no way Becca's going to step aside and let Kami take the role . . .